THE SPACED-OUT SKID STEER

A NOVELLA

WILLIAM CORFF

The Spaced-out Skid Steer

A novella

ISBN: 9798355482817

INTRODUCTION

What would you do if a group of girls in need arrive at your home?

This work of fiction is about the process of an older ranching couple caring for four girls whose troubles follow them from their home world.

My wife and I are not the older couple in the book.

The names of the people and animals have been changed to protect the innocent, but the animals are real. That is, I do live on a ranch with my wife. We have animals we care for. Each one has their own character.

Jack the border collie is a total photo bomber, as apparently many border collies are.

Dan is a beautiful, sweet buckskin boy bred for

dressage. Austin City Limits is a very nice palomino with jumping breeding.

Elise and Donika are big Trakehner broodmares.

It is my sincerest hope that you enjoy this story as a piece of entertainment in a world of many challenges.

William Corff

July 2022

CHAPTER 1

AN UNEXPECTED VISITOR

Old farmers are not generally considered sexy, unless by the old farmer's wife. Thank God. Saves me loads of grief.

Yeah, you have to use sex to get people's attention these days. Farming is pretty much a loner sport. Get up early, milk the cow, gather the eggs, feed the cows, horses, goats, chickens, etc. Got to grease the tractor and implements of the day, check the fluids on the tractor. Get the days fun done.

I was not expecting visitors. Geez when it gets close to dark, I am ready to stop the chores and go in. Well, still have to feed the dogs. I feel my lucky buffalo nickel hanging on my chest getting cool as it does when the barometer starts falling. I take a look around the sky, dark wall cloud rolling from the southwest. A last weather check of the day, definitely some rough weather coming, soon.

Sorry, rambling old farmer, what I was trying to say, I was just going in after another long day, and the dogs start going off. Not the coyote bark, not the neighbor making a beer run bark, not the wilder cougar stay away bark, no. It was the, hey I don't know what you are but don't come too close bark. They are good at talking that way. It is what I pay them for (you know, kibble with left over milk).

"Conner", he is my big Anatolian shepherd, "good boy. " I stepped out past the security light so I could see out in the pasture. There, coming slow, low, and dark with just a little hum it was. I waved at it and pointed to turn past the round pen as if I was waving in an airplane. They pulled right in and parked the thing. I am thinking, must be some CIA thing or Area 51 experimental craft, looked like a bus sized black ovoid. No tires just hovering. My brave dogs are all standing behind me barking. Cannot hear myself think for the racket. I yell to the idiots, "Job done." Then like the good guys they are, they quiet down to a mild growl and watch.

Next a mild glow forms in front of me and a holographic man appears. I ask, "What can I do to help you?"

Holographic man says, "We had a little breakdown and need to get this thing inside before the rain."

I answer, "Got some room in the hay barn. Why don't you pull that thing on in, just follow me." Here I am thinking it must be an experimental craft and wondering if they were flying out of Tinker Airforce Base or out of the one at Enid.

Holographic man answers, " No go bro. You got something to give us a pull with?"

"I have a blue 52-horse tractor and an 82-horse skid steer with lights." I say.

Holographic man says, "Let's try the skid steer."

"Fine. I will go fire her up, but she takes a minute to warm up." I answer as I walk down to the barn to get the skid steer. After turning on the light in the barn, I jump in the skid steer and turn the key and she starts up and then squeals her usual protest at having to work again. I see holographic man standing about 10 feet in front as I sit. I step out to talk with him while I am waiting for the turbocharger bearing to get enough oil flow to stop the squeal. I walk up to him and say, " I have the hay spikes on it now, but I can put the forks on in just a minute. "

He says, "That would be good."

Just then the skid steer dies. I knew I had at least a half tank of fuel in her, so think that is odd. I start walking to her to see what is going on, when she revs to life again but with a quiet hum. I think, "Okay." It takes me a few minutes to drop the bale spikes and put on the pallet forks. Holographic man then tells me to spread the forks wide. "Right oh," says I.

I drive up to the middle of the craft and see slots for the forks, which I gently slip the forks into and lift. The back end of my skid steer rises up a little. It feels like I am lifting about a one ton round bale, but I still have steering and then gently take the thing inside the barn. I put it down, back up the skid steer a bit and flip off the lights. I step out of the skid steer and close the double doors on the barn.

Holographic man lets out a big sigh. The metal of the barn is starting to drum with raindrops. I say, "Hey if you guys need anything let me know. My tools are in the bins on the north wall. " I point to the row of green shipping bins I got from a government auction. Sorry, about the mess though. It has been very difficult to find time to organize them well. Also, if you need anything else, use the phone, or a bite to eat let my wife and I know and by the way, my name is Bill. What would you like me to call you?"

Holographic man looks at me, amazement in his eyes. I am thinking, what kind of government pilot is going to react with surprise when an old farmer offers to help. He finally answers, "Harold. Thank you, thank you so much."

I say, "Welcome." As I step out the side door and head for the house to spend a few minutes with the wife before heading to bed.

CHAPTER 2

GETTING TO MEET THE "BOYS"

The next morning, the ground was soaked, and animals needed feed, and checking. I had loaded the milking stanchion with alfalfa the night before and so I milked the cow at the milking station at the end of the stall barn. I then took the milk in to Deborah to filter, bottle, and put in the fridge. Then I gathered eggs for breakfast and checked the rain gauge before going back in the house. Then with the sunup good, I went into to the hay barn. My spoiled horses like a bit of alfalfa in the morning. The sun was up, and it was getting warm. The thermal mass in the barn was keeping it relatively cool. I opened the door. The guys with that weird craft had been busy.

My usual clutter of tools and bins and rags covered with dust had somehow gotten organized, cleaned up and hung up. "Wow, Harold this is great." I said. Then at my right peripheral vision I saw something. I saw on some square bales what looked like a red-haired model out of a fashion magazine in scanty almost see-through outfit. My first thought was that cannot be comfortable in this barn with the stalks of hay sticking in her feet. Then to her right I saw a dark-haired teen girl in another scanty outfit, not leaving much to the imagination and then further up the haystack was a blond. I said, "What are you doing here. Are you trying to prank me? If you are looking for a job the cabaret is about 30 miles away in the city. " The red-haired gal comes slinking toward me as the other two follow. They come close with the red-haired gal in front, the dark haired one to my right, the blond to my left, and more modestly dressed brown haired girl with brilliant eyes. I say, "It really must hurt your feet walking barefooted on this hay and gravel."

The red-haired gal looks at me surprised and talks. Harold the holographic man appears and translates in her voice. She says, "Can you believe him, he actually is concerned about our feet." Then Harold translates the blond. "But we saw the pens in the other barn."

At that point I cut in, "The pens in the other barn are stalls for my horses. I will be happy to introduce you to them, but you will need to be dressed better. Besides if my wife sees me with you girls dressed like this it will be very bad for me. "

The brunette talks and Harold translates, "He speaks of his wife as if he only has one. Does he not find us attractive? Perhaps his wife is also male?"

I say, "Look, girls you are very attractive, and my wife is a female. You also look as if you are old enough to be my granddaughters. I also love my wife. Who are you and why are you here? Is this some kind of prank? What happened to the government guys with the experimental vehicle?"

The four girls start talking with each other and Harold is translating away rapid fire as they talk about pens and slave girls/sex slaves and escaping from their handler and what are they going to wear when they only have their exhibit outfits left and now that the vehicle is partly fixed they could try to sneak back to, but where would they go and not be caught and how they were supposed to be the entertainment for some kind of victory party.

"Wow, girls if you need some kind of help other than vehicle repair, need clothes etc, let me get my wife out here and you talk with her." I turn, walk out the door back into the sunlight. I shake my head, take a breath and walk back to the house. I ask my wife to come with me out to the barn. She asks, "Why?". I tell her there are some women there who had vehicle trouble and they might be interested in horses. My wife's passion in life is horses. She can talk horse for hours. She comes with me out to the hay barn. I open the door and in she goes. I escape back to the house to pretend I am looking for a tractor part online.

So, after doing a load of laundry, sharpening all the knifes in the house, putting the dishes away out of the dishwasher, scrubbing the floors, dusting the bookshelves, cleaning the bathrooms they all come in. Okay I did not scrub the floors, dust the bookshelves or clean the bathrooms but I did change the sheets on the guest room beds and clear the dishes off the table. They are still talking full bore and Harold the holograph is translating in rapid female talk.

Deborah, my wife, leads them into what had been my daughter's bedroom and old clothes are flying out of drawers and the closet. I am thinking this is not a safe place for me. So, I go out and play ball and stick with Jack my border collie. Then I go out to put the brush hog on the tractor and go mow the front pasture. That keeps the weeds and brush down, helps the grass, and breaks up the manure piles left by the cows and horses. Around lunch time I head back in covered with the usual dust and pollen. The girls are all covered up now, so further exposure will have to be the stuff of dreams. It is best that way. The girls and my wife are still talking but now, Deborah is actually cooking a full meal, not just heating stuff out of the freezer in the microwave. Ah the perks of having company.

Some people think an old country boy is just a stupid hick. Being one, I think that is hilarious. I chose to live in the country. Raising animals, one learns that they need careful changes in diet or else great discomfort or worse can happen. So, guess what guys, these girls were in for a world of hurt unless, yes my wife wisely provided probiotics and small portions. They still raved about the food. They speak of ration sticks they have been eating which apparently after a few days were truly monotonous. Deborah soaked in the praise. Don't get me wrong, I always appreciate her cooking and tell her so, but the effort invested has sort of waned over the last few years with just us at home.

Amazingly, I was starting to understand more and more of what they were saying without translation. That was when I heard them tell Deborah that if I had not been so nice when I met them, something they did not really expect, they would have killed me and taken over the farm. Deborah promptly told them that she was glad they did not do so.

CHAPTER 3

THE LIFE OF BARBARA

Girls sometimes have to grow up quick. My parents nurtured and loved me so very much and I will always miss them. Oh, to get that hug. Mom and dad had seen the distortion and perversion of media manipulation with lies and erosion of culture and life. I was too young to understand. They had been free to do their research when they met. Now they were becoming more and more slaves of those in power in the "name of the better good". The said to each other in private the people in power were the ones getting the goods. They had watched how laws were passed that applied to the people but exempted the politicians making them. It seemed that few noticed or maybe they were too cowed to protest. My parents had been brilliant, young, respected, and given freedom with their work until elections had rolled in the "New Hope" regime. Turned accountable respected systems gone to lies, disinformation, corruption,... but enough. It was all a well-used system by the Bihaddi to gain control, bring in their perverted culture and religion, and enslave us all.

Mom and dad were not happy. They aligned their research to assist in an underground revolt. The use of AI to aid in communication between species was not considered a core vital aspect of the revolt's needs but it was vital for me. Seeing how young girls were being taken from homes as toys for the Bihaddi pleasure, they implanted their genius into me. Implanted into my neural network and DNA. At least that is what I have found so far.

I was taken from my parents by the Bihaddi when 9 1/2. Like so many other girls I would never see my parents again. Seems their Initiator chose his youngest sex slave/wife at about that age. The slaver thought me a special case given the genius of my parents and how I would fit into the Bihaddi breeding program. There was a significantly greater price paid for virgins who could provide genius potential. I was groomed to be sold for the big money. They did not think I needed any education beyond care for my master's needs.

I was trained in domestic care, cooking, house

care, sexual prowess, child rearing the Bihaddi way. What they did not see was the instruction my parents had built into their implant. They did not see how I was being educated by my parent's loving legacy. They did see how I would separate myself from the other girls and sit quietly. They did not see how I was learning so much of the history, science, culture of our world. They did not see how I was developing the ability to touch and interact with the AI systems in the facility. I knew to keep the appearance of subservience. I knew to learn, to grow, to connect, to mature, and have hope. I hoped I would have the time to grow and mature and connect to the point of having an escape from the hell of the Bihaddi.

In our culture Hope was an angel called upon in times of great need. My need was great. Again, I would sit quietly, listen and process the WiFi traffic. I began to be able to translate code and then to interact. I did not know what to learn at first. I could read where the data flow was going. I followed the date flow, learning source code. So many of the other girls in the facility were slated for "special harems" for the Bihaddi warriors. I called them social whore houses and felt sorry for the poor girls. I was so lonely though. There were none there whom I felt safe talking with. This drove me to read the reports by the matrons at the different training centers as they came on line.

In the reports I learned fate. The fate of the girls enslaved. The fate of my peers being groomed for sale to the richer Bihaddi. I learned there was no escape on this world. I learned how the Bihaddi shipped girls back to their own world for the "pleasure palaces". I learned how the condition of poor girls who were sent back to be reconditioned after they said enough. I observed our poor matrons who though overseeing us, had their own histories. There were little grunts and moans at times as they moved, some bent over. The poor lady assigned to care for me would have drops of blood oozing from her back at times soaking through her garments. I learned I absolutely did not want to continue feeding male Bihaddi's sick appetites with myself. My mother had had seen these things coming. She had given me a plan. I would need help, though. That is when I began scanning the reports in earnest. I needed other capable smart girls who were highly motivated. I needed a spaceship and a space to escape to. A place to warn of the evil coming. A plan to defeat that evil. I was praying for that angel, Hope so hard each night to help me.

Even after I found girls, in different parts of our world I thought would be good assets to my plan, how was I going to get in touch with them and get them to me and have all hardware together to make our space vehicle? Fortunately, I was now in the elite training facility for girls on out planet to be shipped to the Bihaddi home planet. All "elite" girls were brought here first for finishing before their shipment. Thus, it was I watched as my soon to be dear friends were transported as precious cargo to my facility. There was Alana, of the dark skin from our middle planet continent. She was the first. She was quiet and morose when I first saw her. We were not allowed to talk at first. Quarantine was strictly adhered to by the matrons. I saw her get online on a tiny tablet she had secreted on the journey with her. I was to later learn it was actually implanted into her skin on her arm. A gift from her father who was an engineer. I tapped into it. Introduced myself. She was surprised and suspicious at first. As I would have been. I had read her report about how she was found many times making neat working toy models of vehicles for the younger girls. These delighted the girls, but the matrons were confused about how to handle this prodigy. I knew just what I needed. I needed her. I began giving her diagrams and instructions about how to make the different vehicles I could scrounge up online. She devoured these. Surreptitiously of course. The matrons would have shut us down immediately if they found out. I had no picture of myself except from younger times until I found my own report and description in the matrons' documents. It was with that I introduced myself finally to her. She said, "Oh that is you."

As I was cultivating Alana, I also saw another special girl coming to our facility. Hermosa was from the far island archipelago on the other side of our world. She seemed to have a hot temper that could flare up and burn those about her and then subside. Her red hair went well with those flames. It was funny to me how the matrons seemed excited about the value of this hotblooded girl. She was bigger boned than Alana or I. She was also reported to have an intuition about herbs and plants and their healing that pleased the matrons. Contacting her was a bit trickier as plant communication skills ran to the fractal. I mean I could manipulate a plant to bud out fractal bits but to get it to warp into a message, that was stretching me. Thank God, mom and dad had thought that growing things might be a necessary survival skill. Thus, I met Hermosa as I tended a garden, I had volunteered to help my matron with the spices needed for cooking.

The matron was so pleased as this made me more valuable. I was able to shed little DNA particles with massages on Hermosa's plants. Somehow, she detected these and translated them. It gave her a connection to me. She is so incredibly psychic. When finally, I was able to touch her in the garden as she reached for one her plants, she was shocked and pleased at the connection and we have been sharing visions of our worlds since. She is the most sensitive person I have ever known. I knew, then as now, that her anger was always at some part of life being needlessly hurt by actions of a person. Her hatred of the Bihaddi was profound. She was also pleased to learn of Alana and our little click of rebels.

Now we had friends, but what were we to do to escape the finished shipment we were slated for. We were each 11 now. Soon our menses would flow, and the matrons would be looking more closely at shipping us to the dreaded Bihaddi home planet.

I had been doing my best to search out space vehicles and the needs for these and survival requirements. I also came across some oblique references to antigravitational devices that had been perfected on a previous planet the Bihaddi captured and raped. The Bihaddi had captured some of these but there were references to more complex and better controlled models they had not been able to capture or even understand the destroyed vehicles left behind at the Bihaddi invasion. I managed to peruse the plans the Bihaddi used in their space vehicles. But more interesting were the small vehicular plans stored in an obscure file about old foreign technologies. One chapter on antigravitational insects. Okay, many of your large beetles are too heavy to be able to get enough lift from their miniscule wings. On the undersurface of their hard wings were found these cones that when recreated in larger size provided an antigravitational lift which enabled the beetles to fly quite well.

I forwarded the information to Alana. She was so excited and began immediately little experiments to recreate a working model. Finding supplies for experimentation was a challenge. I found a document on our facility describing a garage where ancient automobiles, tools and other equipment were stored. She wanted to go immediately. I had to warn her to wait until dark hours when the matrons slept. Sneaking out the compound was especially risky. We would need to create another access to the garage as a working area. The northeast wall was contiguous with the garage. We found an approximate location of what used to be a doorway access to it that had been bricked up and then stuccoed over. This was in what was now a hallway to dining area. How were we to use it for access without obvious change to the existing wall?

There was so much to get done, to learn, and all

to be kept secret. I prayed for the angel of Hope to help our little band with every breath. Then Hermosa told me of a family she had read about before the take over who lived on the cold southern continent. They were robotics experts. There was mention in the article of a younger daughter. Where was she, we wondered.

Then the next shipment of girls came in. I read the matron's reports. Zoe was a special southern girl. She was blond, highly intelligent, with the fair skinned oval face of the southerners. She was a year younger than us, but her blond fair skinned features were highly valued. She was a bit of an unknown to us. How would I vet her or even contact her? We found they had actually given her robotic tools and equipment because she had made robotic toys that the kids and the elite loved, and the matrons and slavers could ship off and sell. Thus, a crash course in robotics was my next challenge.

Poor little Zoe. The matrons were working her for hours and hours making the toys. She was on a whole other level in the facility than I. Finally, I was able to realize she had a battery recharging system in her room that she would be changing batteries in daily. Knowing the timing of when she would change these was the challenge. If I timed it right, I might be able to contact her via wired surface direct contact with her neural structures. I tried first in the morning. Nothing. Then I tried in the evening. I felt a contact. I could tell she felt it too. But it scared her. I tried to calm her. She let go too fast.

I kept checking morning, noon, and night. It was two days before I made contact again. This time more gently. I told her who I was and that I was just another girl in the facility, and I wanted to talk to her, and this was the only way I could. She asked tentatively if I was wanting one of the toy robots. "No" I said, "I want to know you." Zoe said, "But I am just another girl in the facility." I said, "No you are not. You are Zoe Farmer and you father was a famous robotics expert." She said, "Yes that is me. How do you know who I am, and what does it matter with the Bihaddi ruling everything?" I tell her, "I think you need to meet my friends."

Hope is born of the sense of a chance to better your life. When Zoe met Alana, Hermosa, and I she cried tears of joy. She had lost all hope and was going through the motions making her toys. She had seen her brother killed by the Bihaddi when he had tried to protect her with his robots from capture. They had previously picked up her parents "as needed by the state". Her brother was 8 years older than her, and she idolized him, and he doted on her. We had found a way to sneak into Zoe's room while the rest of the facility slept. We quietly hugged her as the drone of matron snores echoed in the hallway. As I touched each one, they felt the neural connection and I felt my mother's implant touch each through my fingers and give them an input I did not then understand. It was after that we shared a communication, a wireless network we would silently work to create our escape.

CHAPTER 4

WORKING WHILE THE CLOCK IS TICKING

Friends to share life with, share purpose with secretly was sweet but we lived in constant fear. Zoe finally worked out making a robot to make the simple toys with the help of parts tooled and snuck in by Alana. Alana came up with a plan to create a covered cupboard at the area of the hidden door to the garage where some of Zoe's robotic toys could be housed for the matrons and other girls to play with. This of course would have to be approved by the head matron but with a bit of begging by the other girls to see and play with the toys. Thus, with some manipulation off the matrons with a diagram of the cupboard by Alana and offer by her to build the cupboard with intricate designs to show off her skills, this was approved. What was not in the diagram was the attachment to the wall with hidden opening to garage door after removal of the stucco. To the matrons this was a win-win providing a venue to show off the value of two of their charges with the cupboard and the toys in one place.

Alana was working on the anti-gravitation and thrust experimentation for the vehicle we needed. Hermosa was working on life support in the vehicle air, food, water, and plant life to take with us, at least as seeds. Zoe was working on construction of the vehicle by making robots to do the heavy work, forming the vehicle, helping Alana. I was keeping each of us in touch with the other, monitoring the matrons and the doings of the Bihaddi and researching where we would go.

Mom and dad had tried to give me the totality of the knowledge they had available. In their own way this had been given to Alana, Hermosa, and Zoe. Sharing that was huge, but it was not enough. I was starting to tap into the deeper archives of the Bihaddi. In our facility training we were indoctrinated how great and generous were the Bihaddi were. We were to worship the Bihaddi warriors and be subservient to them in every way. We were told of their great history of service to peoples bringing the poor ignorant masses the true culture and religion and how grateful the people were for their liberation from ignorance.

Having seen the "liberation" from our "ignorant cultures" we would just smile our little knowing smiles as we kept our heads down so the matrons would not see. Some work on metal cannot be done totally quietly, we found. So, Zoe made a robot who excavated a cavern for continued work. Zoe also made some minuscule robots who went into the kitchens and secured food for us to prepare for our journey. Hermosa created ways for it to last while we were making our journey. We did not know how long we would be getting to whatever destination we would be going to. I was continuing to monitor the Bihaddi as best I could. I seemed to be getting better at it as I was now getting the plans to their weapons and tactics for invasion and their real history.

The pressing issue was that we were getting older, and the matrons were starting to give us appraising looks. Out bodies were starting to change shape, getting wider at the hip and filling in the breast. A tight wrap around the chest might hide some breast tissue but hips are a bigger challenge. So far no one had gone into the old garage but that would not hold if we went into hiding. Also, construction of our craft was starting to need more materials than we had available in the near area.

They would be wanting to ship us off soon. It was critical that we stay together. Zoe created a digger robot to tunnel a passage to a cavern I had located on an old geologic survey. This would be a good location for us. We still had to have food, water, our equipment and things and the ability to get more things as needed. It was also imperative that we leave no clues of our escape. We still needed freedom to work our plans. We needed to disappear in a way they would not be looking for us. The courtyard would be a safe place we could be seen together. We would have a 100-foot sink hole open up under us and they would see us fall with massive dust rising up as it opened up underneath us. Then we would disappear. It would not be worth their trouble to try to find us buried at the bottom of the hole when they presumed, we were already dead. There had been an old well that had been filled in in the courtyard. Our robot laborer would excavate the hole with a platform to hold the top together until needed. We would fall a few feet onto a platform that would then retract and close hiding us as a cloud of dust rose obscuring all.

Well, that was the plan.

CHAPTER 5

THE HOLE TRUTH

I was picking up chatter between the matrons and their overseers of an upcoming invasion and the need for trophies for warriors. Trophies! I valued my life a lot more than as an award on a shelf. I certainly did not want to let my little blue-eyed self be sold so. The robots were digging but the dirt had to go somewhere. We had cleared out the old garage with all the equipment. The robot digger was filling that up fast. We would have to explore our cavern more for a dumping place while sealing up the escape hatch, we would fall to when the hole opened. Poor Zoe was feeling overwhelmed struggling to keep her robots working with the limited resources we had and the wear and abrasion from dirt. We were needing more supplies. We were needing them fast. Oh yeah just go buy what you need. Hmmm. What money? Who to do the buying? Us in our little harem outfits? Even if Zoe had the resources, she did not have the time to create a humanoid for us. Hiring a local who would not betray us? Extremely risky. I had holographic memories of my dad to help me remember him. Could I use those? With Alana and Zoe, we built a portable holographic video projector, and I programmed the dialogue and video. Now we just needed a way to pay for the supplies we needed.

Alana thought we should search the whole of the cavern so we could find buried treasure. This resulted in some arguments about time, cave ins, resources, probability, and what treasure are you talking about. Hermosa thought we could trade herbs and plants. Okay, Hermosa who knows about your potions and plants and would be willing to trade for, or buy them? Zoe thought she could make more toy robots. She was already too busy with the hole escape and her toys were known. It would expose our deception. I told them I would tap into the financial data flow and see if there was a way we could get funds undetected. Once I deciphered the data flow, starting with the nearby bank transfers, I found I could create a fictitious account. It was then pretty simple to just add fractional digits to the transactions and then siphon them to my account. I set the type font for my account to so minuscule and light it should be invisible to the normal eye on computer page or print. I could then follow the digital financial flow and add more income streams to flow to my account.

Thus, we were able to order our supplies and pay for them to be delivered. Searching town maps and tax ledgers I found there were numerous empty houses out on the edge of town. I searched for secluded locations supplies could be delivered to and found a couple of good ones. That way I could have deliveries to multiple locations and then have a robotic pick up after a holographic greeting of the delivery agent.

The ability to acquire needed resources gave Zoe greater freedom in robotic creation and speeded up our preparations for escape. I had started menstruating and was struggling to keep this from the matron. I was doing my best to avoid her. I knew her fairly well now. Her grimace when she bent over was from scars on her back from lashes. I had begun to wonder how she would miss me when I was gone. She treated me like a daughter. The matrons did try to keep use well fed and instructed according to their prejudices. It was still slavery. I did not wish them ill but did not want to continue in their traditions.

When I was cleaning up the financial account and programming to continue to remain hidden, I decided to transfer the excess moneys we had siphoned off to the matron's accounts. I doubted they would tell anyone despite not knowing its origin and it would be a great blessing to them. I knew they had suffered much and maybe this would salve some of what they had suffered under the Bihaddi.

It was getting urgent to escape and not everything was ready. The hole was dug. The escape hatch in the side was ready along with closing in. Clothing and mannequins were strategically placed at the bottom of the hole but there was no time for a retracting platform to be in place. We had to get going. We had to improvise. We created a micro-hook bed, something like Velcro, we would fall on and then retract into our escape hatch, which would then close and fill with dirt. We wore special clothes the micro-hooks would catch on. What we did not know was when the dirt whooshed up with the hole opening how much of it went onto the micro-hook platform and how close we were to losing little Zoe. I managed to hold her with one hand while grasping the micro-hook platform with the other. Alana fell almost totally into the escape hatch with Hermosa falling on her. The retraction happened fast, and we were laying together in the dark. I felt warm fluid on my hand on the micr0-

hooks. When in our escape tunnel and the dust cleared, I could see the blood oozing in the dirt on my hand.

CHAPTER 6

DUSTING OFF FOR TAKEOFF

Though we had escaped and thought our ruse was good enough to have the matrons think we were dead, there was still the chance that that might change, or our existence otherwise be discovered. We felt a need to hurry our departure. Hermosa kindly and lovingly treated my wounded hand but it was still painful for many days while we were finishing the space craft. I picked up data traffic about a planet that was broadcasting complex signals indicating intelligent, even human life. They had found the exact location some 20 years ago and been infiltrating but were not fully ready for invasion yet. Indications were that this was a lesser advanced civilization and would soon be ready for the Bihaddi. Plans were being put together for a fleet to invade and conquer. They were using their usual divide to conquer efforts via the political and media systems. The system worked for them if they were just patient and let the system have time to work, as it had done so many times before.

The Bihaddi had plans for conquering this new world, but as we talked, we wondered if those people would repeat the capitulation of our own world if there was proper warning and preparation of adequate defense. We hoped we could make a difference for ourselves and for this world. Finally, our vehicle was ready, and we had ourselves ready with much information of Bihaddi equipment, tactics, and space vehicles. I had profiles on each of their commanders and officers.

In our cavern all was ready to go but we needed access to open sky. There was an opening that provided air flow out in the desert. It had to be enlarged for us to get above ground. As the robots enlarged the opening, it became clear the boulders were unstable around the opening when one crashed in and destroyed our largest robot excavator. When that boulder was removed, we were able use the remains of that large robot as roof support and squeeze out in the fresh air. Finally, out on open ground we did final assessments of all aspects of our vehicle.

With the impending takeoff, I scheduled a

programmed viral overload of local monitoring systems to give us a window of time to go unobserved. Once we reached space, we continued using our moon to slingshot us out of the system and begin our journey. The close swing round the moon threw us in a very rapid trajectory to the largest planet where we slid round to the side hidden from the home planet where we could make our hyperdrive jump to the destination solar system. Hyperdrive jumps tended to create an energetic flash observant monitors might pick up.

CHAPTER 7

SUN ABOVE FIRE BELOW

Not much to see on a hyperdrive jump. Data coming in was undecipherable. One set course to a star and if transport had been at that system before, one had orbital data on all planets and asteroids. We did not have this. We were in transit and with a prayer we would arrive in open space in an outer planetary void. During the days of transit, we shared stories of our lives and dreams before the Bihaddi. We had to restrict food to essential nutrition. Urine we could recycle to palatable water. Fecal matter we had to store. To flush it into space could be fatal as it slammed into you when you decelerated. Shitty way to go.

Hermosa talked about growing herbs during our trip. She tried a few. Weight considerations had stopped her from bringing any of her well-loved plants. They sprouted up to two leaves by the time we were decelerating. When we came out to free fall and were finally able to take local readings the poor seedlings started vibrating to the point they fell apart. That with the nausea we were feeling was very upsetting. We came in opposite side the orbit of the largest planet and mapped a gentle approach down to the inhabited planet. We were getting a lot of transmitted traffic now from there and doing our best to decipher it. This was a great distraction that caused us to not have our shields all the way up as we came down to the planets moon. It was there we got the warning clarion of a detecting bot scanning our vehicle. We jettisoned the fecal matter and put on full cloaking, hoping to cause target confusion. It seemed to work as we were able to continue but a whole load of pooh flashed into nonexistence.

As we were now in earth's gravity well and passively falling, tracking us would be most unlikely. We desperately needed allies on this strange planet and were each scouring through transmissions and started to be able to interact with what they called wireless internet. We needed a place to settle, a place where we could hide our craft, and a place we could continue research and development of a defense against the coming invasion.

CHAPTER 8

TELL ME AGAIN PLEASE

Learning you have aliens from another planet in your house takes a moment to process. Well, they surely did not feel alien, well maybe, since they were beautiful, interested, hardworking, kind, considerate, and tough. It is with purpose, striving, and achievement that one blooms to fruit of being. The Bihaddi thought they owned them, but they had won a passage to new life with us. We fostered exchange students before who came to learn American English but mostly to spend time with horses. It was a bit of a stretch for us in our little house to have four girls. They seemed content. The clutter of years, by necessity, was cleared out of the house. My tools and workshop were now almost organized. Their vehicle was gradually disappearing into pieces. The only visitors that came out to our place were UPS and FedEx. So, keeping the girls' presence unremarkable given our history of exchange students and horses should be relatively easy, that is unless they went to into town. Deborah and I lived on a fairly tight budget, but we were happy to share what we had. Besides the bloom of purpose was back on Deborah's face and I was finally getting more done on the place than just basics.

Deborah and I knew things were screwy in our world and had retreated to our farm knowing we were just "little people" in the world. The media and powers seemed to be bent on destruction of our freedoms, culture, and lifestyle. The levers we had seemed just too small to fit the fulcrum to right the skewed "normal" of the "modern" world. Our lever was love and our animals thrived. Just too few knew our value or touch.

CHAPTER 9

A HOUSE FULL OF GIRLS AND A BARN FULL OF HORSES

My wife and I had talked seriously about retiring from the horse business. We had some nice stallions and good broodmares but were getting a bit up there. It was getting harder for me to get all the chores done. She basically stuck to the house except for little emergencies or things. She had a bum knee that would try to give out on her and had not been able to ride in years. I had more than I could do each day trying to keep the place up and take care of the horses. I now had arthritis in my right leg and foot from fractures acquired over the years. Some from collecting stallions (getting their semen for artificial insemination breeding) and having them rear to the collecting phantom dancing on two feet while I am under them putting on the AV (artificial vagina) for the collection.

When that 1300-pound animal's hoof lands on your foot, something gives. Deborah had even posted and advertised that we were retiring and selling down our stock.

We had tried hiring but found too often either they thought the pay too little, even with housing and food and decided they would augment it with some light finger acquisitions and leave. We even had one fellow kill a very fine horse and steal a saddle and bridle before leaving. It was time for us to retire.

Then these four girls show up. Deborah loves nothing more than to nurture children except maybe to talk horse. Deborah and I had questions but with a little patience and listening those get answered. It is kind of like training a fine horse, give a little nudge in the right direction and praise when they move that way. A light touch, a little tug to give direction and release and praise when that direction is taken. With good breeding and an early start, it is a relatively easy task. The later the start, the poorer the breeding, the more difficult the task.

The girls were very curious about the horses. If you know horses, you know each one has a personality. We had been careful over the years to breed for willing sweet personalities in our horses. I introduced a few of my young boys. I put Austin City Limits (a 2-year-old palomino Trakehner thorough bred mix stallion) first in the stalks (a four posted stand with side bars and gates on either end to help keep the horse contained when working with it) and had each girl take a grooming brush and brush him down. You could almost hear him purr with all the attention. We then took him out to the round pen, and I showed them basics on lunging.

He kicked up a little at first but settled and we did about 7 minutes first right then left. We talked about the techniques we used to teach each horse manners and strengthen it and how to communicate with a horse and some of the different disciplines with horses. Of course, Jack, our border collie had to photobomb everything by chasing around the round pen like a maniac until I finally snagged him and put him in in an empty stall to remove his mischievous distraction.

The girls were absorbing the whole experience. Then I allowed Barbara to hold the lead rope for leading Austin. I explained how he was a bit of a naughty boy and kept escaping from his pen where he would be kept with the other 2-year-old boys. She smiled a very pretty smile with this and started to pet him on the neck and he started to nuzzle and lick her hand. With stallions it is wise to be wary of bites. It is natural for them to bite the neck of a mare when they breed. Since I had raised him from foaling, I had never observed him bite a person, but he would lick someone he liked. I was a little surprised though when she dropped the rope and started walking that he followed her keeping shoulder to shoulder. Barbara was beaming at this point.

Deborah was out now talking horse with the girls so I made a quick exit and mucked Austin's stall so it would be ready for his return. When the weather is nice, I prefer to keep the horses out in pasture. That way they can eat grass, be with their buddies, play and run with their buddies, and I have less expense in bedding, and less work in mucking. When young horses play and run, they build cartilage and I think stay healthier.

After Barbara brought in Austin, Alana wanted to work with Dan. Dan is a bigger bodied 1-year-old buckskin Trakehner thoroughbred stallion. Basically, he is a sweet boy. She seemed stouter than Barbara and Dan and her hit it off well. Then she started asking me about how the lighting worked in the barn? What did each tool do? How did the skid steer work? Etc., etc, Okay I did my best to explain each piece of equipment taking her for a walk after Dan was put away. I showed her the tractor and each of the implements explaining a little about what each was for and how they were used. I do not think she was getting everything she wanted, so I suggested a trip to the computer where I showed her how to access videos and text on different pieces of equipment. I showed her online repair manuals I had for the skid steer and tractor.

Then I also told her there was a patent office where one could access inventions of all types of ideas people had had. She was lost to me after that for many hours. I think she finally looked up when Deborah called us to dinner.

Hermosa had seen alfalfa in the barn when we first met and had picked up a piece of it. She asked me what it was and noted how we fed it out to animals. She spread it out on the guest room desk noting the leaf spacing and how the stems grew. She then pulled from a pouch she always wore, a piece of Bermuda grass and asked what it was. Then she pulled out some thistle, ragweed, crab grass, and queen Anne's lace. I took her to an old laptop computer and showed her how to search for the different grasses, herbs, weeds, and trees local to our area. At that point I seemed to no longer exist in the room, so I quietly exited to get back to chores.

Miss Zoe, I had learned was a year younger than the other girls. She had been working with Deborah who had shown her all the kitchen gadgets. Then she noted the clutter of my desk. My desk has been relegated to a back room away from the rest of what most people see of the house. Something about having a position in the center of tools, parts and pieces, nuts, bolts, batteries, a small torch, levels, my glasses for reading, an old calculator, and old desktop computers parked in the corner. I think she lit up the most when she saw that. I asked if she would like to see the rest of my tools and told her she was welcome to use them as long as I got them back when I needed them. If she needed any parts she was welcome to them especially the old stuff I had been putting off taking apart or discarding. That was a hug I will never forget. Old men are not supposed to tear up over some little kid, are they?

CHAPTER 10

SETTLING IN

The girls' appetites were getting bigger as they were now doing some of the chores. Having the stalls mucked and those horses fed and groomed with leading lessons helped a lot. The girls were now starting to talk to the horse assigned to them. I would catch snatches of conversation but chose not to listen too closely. Private conversations, you know. Deborah was giving each girl riding lessons on our reliable mares, Elise and Donika. Each girl seemed a natural, but Barbara was advancing almost faster than Deborah could teach. Deborah thought advancing to some of the calm pregnant mares would be the next safe step. The girls had now mastered the art of charming the horses and leading them. A horse cookie can go a long way to helping catch a lazy nag. Sweet talk and horse massages also helped set a relationship. Deborah was a stickler for consistency in your conversation with a horse. You talked with your ride with your body, posture, leg movements, fingers lightly moving reins, balance, not just voice. You listened to the horse watching ear position, head position, tension, accepting the bit, etc. With them able to take care of basics that freed me to go do the brush hogging and brush cutting. I even was able to repair some fencing. After her lesson Alana walked out into the pasture to see what I was doing. I explained to her the basics of freeing a broken post pulling the U-nails and hot wire connectors, then digging up the old post part in the ground. I explained how I painted the bottom of the post before putting it the ground, showed her how to use a post hole digger and to make the 2 ½ foot deep hole (our soil is red Oklahoma clay so a deeper hole is needed when it rains and gets soft) and then resetting the new post leveling it and tamping the back fill sequentially to get a nice tight rigid set post.

It was later I found Ms. Alana and Zoe in the shop working on some sort of machine. I asked if they had everything they needed. I was not prepared for that answer. Aluminum, titanium, wiring, circuit boards, heat source, cutting lasers, etc., etc. "Okay, girls", I said, "let me show you around the shop, the attic where more of the old computers are, look at some of the old equipment in the old cow barn, and let me show you how to pay online and order what you need.

We have limited funds here, but I am sure Deborah will help you placing any orders." So, a quick tour of the shop introducing the torch, the welder, where the different saws, nippers, wiring and connectors, and nuts, bolts, fasteners, etc. That seemed to help some. Then we went into the attic, and I showed them all the old computers I had put away with all the old power supplies thinking that one day I would extract the gold from them. They seemed excited about all that old junk. Then I took them to Deborah who took over showing them the intricacies of ordering online and the limits of our finances. It was at that point they brought in Barbara and Deborah explained we only had the money we got with retirement and selling our horses and the horse market had been hard on us the last few years.

When I looked at Barbara, I saw a very beautiful brown haired blue eyed girl with a very winning smile. I could see her listen intently when in conversation. She seemed to need more quiet time and would sit in contemplative mode for long periods. She was a natural leader and the girls all recognized her as such. When confronted with the fact of our limited finances she smiled and said something about bit coin mining. At that point I saw a rapid egress from the room. The girls set up a dust free zone in my workshop. They brought down every old computer, power supply, fan, air conditioner, old cell phones, TVs, radios, blenders, and other bits and pieces and were busy for the next few days.

During all this Hermosa was either actively scouring the property finding new plants, herbs, and trees to add to her knowledge. She was also working with Deborah in the kitchen or the garden preparing meals or researching medical knowledge.

Of course, there were still chores with horses to take care of and riding lessons and time was taken off for these.

CHAPTER 11

BARBARA'S COOL MONEY

Quiet moments on the farm are precious. Momentous research along information pathways into this new world's solutions to the multitude of problems we beings created. But blue-eyed solutions to the problems, I knew were coming with the Bihaddi, were my goal. I could see they had already infiltrated the mainstream news systems working to divide the people. Create division, corrupt the inner hearts message, make truth the lie and the lie truth, the path to cultural destruction. There is no hero when all are living for their own pleasure. Create problem after problem and have the false solution. Their solution always ended in slavery. My father taught me that I was a soul. A soul on a journey. My life in the universe was my classroom. The soul learns from consequences for its actions. When evil no longer has appropriate consequences, then it festers, and pestilence grows, and suffering becomes the norm.

I had studied the ways of the Bihaddi on my home world and accessed their ships plans and battle plans from the histories they communicated to each other. I had learned there were certain clues and signs of their presence in their electronic communications. I had started seeing some of those here. It would have been easy for them to infiltrate this world. They preferred a soft takeover. They would not be expecting my monitoring. I had yet to work out what I would do with their communications and what I would do to stop their invasion when it came. It seemed there were plenty of good people not wanting the changes they were seeing promoted by the those presenting themselves as the authorities on behavior with their "political correctness". Control the media, Indoctrinate the susceptible, buy-off the political powerful, and destroy the good in the culture was their way. It is amazing how people can convince themselves their view is correct when so much evidence contradicts that belief. I had a dossier on the Bihaddi activities but needed a means to subvert it. I also needed a means to destroy their invasion fleet when it came.

It only took a few days for Alana and Zoe to

perfect and even improve the blueprints I gave them for doing Crypto currency mining. We needed the money and Bill and Deborah needed it as well to help us. With money coming in we could upgrade our currency mining and make more, and with that buy the supplies we would need and upgrade our internet access and plans.

CHAPTER 12

MINING TREASURES

The girls were learning everything extremely fast. We had had an exchange student years ago who stayed the summer to learn American English, but she was really here for the horses. There was now less and less of hologram man as the girls were speaking and understanding American English so well now.

We started to have daily deliveries with the UPS driver, the FEDEX driver, and USPS. I at first was worried our limited finances were being eroded but Barbara assured me that it was all paid for by their bitcoin. I was also seeing innovations in gadgets in the kitchen and now my skid steer quietly fired right up, and I no longer needed to jump the old tractor to get it going. Looking at what their innovations were doing, I suggested to Barbara they could patent new ideas and inventions. Alana and Zoe had been looking at patented inventions for some time. I suggested they might patent some of their ideas but given they were minors legally and wanting to stay well hidden it probably should be done in Deborah's or my name. The government patent office had a site that listed the requirements for filing but patenting could take some time.

Deborah told me that night since it looked like the girls were staying, we would need to register them with the local high school. They would start in the fall of course. I told Deborah there might be some questions about parentage and immigration status and she should talk to the girls about that before going to the high school. Running a ranch of course I had to go into town in the truck and get feed for animals and Deborah would get groceries. Hermosa and Barbara had gone shopping with Deborah at first and been fascinated by process and large selection of items. Hermosa was fascinated with the varieties of produce and clothing. Barbara had checked out the electronics section, but it got a little weird when she touched one of the big screens in the back of the WalMart and her face came on the screen. She removed her hand, and it went back to the normal video.

Deborah said they were clearly looking all

around, and Hermosa remarked how none of the women had to cover their face. The variation in clothing available also was very interesting to them.

Later Deborah also drove by the high school to show them where it was. They saw both boys and girls walking around the school and even some holding hands. Deborah told Barbara and Hermosa about the girl we had as an exchange student years before. She explained how we had a contract with her school and that when registering them the school would need their identification data with address and guardian and contacts for emergencies. Deborah told me there was a thoughtful silence in the truck as they drove home after that.

It was not long after that that when Deborah took the girls to go shopping, they were buying their own clothing and jewelry. They had learned how to convert some of their bitcoin earnings into cash now. It is normal for our electric bill to go down in the late spring before summer heat. I had read that the bit coin mining was a power hog for electricity. Odd I thought but I did not say anything. A couple of weeks later I noted a letter from the patent office in the mail. It was not a week later we got a call from a toy manufacturer.

Someone had seen the patent application and they were very interested. At the dinner table

Deborah and I tried to explain a little bit of contract law where a minor could not legally sign a contract, and this was to protect them. Each of them said their parents were dead. There was an intense sadness in the eyes of each as that was stated going round the table. A few tears began to fall, then more. After some group hugs and a bit of tea and cookies, that storm cleared, and we explained that we could sign for them if we were legal guardians. We explained though that that was typically a process and might take some time.

The letter from the patent office simply said the patent application had been accepted. Deborah and I explained that that gave it a patent pending status but there was a process of verification involving a search of the patents, so we were not replicating an existing one that had been granted. This was, of course, with all the girls at the dinner table.

It was at that point they all started talking at once with Alana talking about an application for a bit miner device that reduced power usage, Hermosa talking about extracting an alkaloid in oat grass that acted as a telomere protector, and Barbara talking about a nano structured molecule that enhanced human animal communication by acting on the brain's neocortex. They had not yet submitted patent applications on these. I said these were great ideas but so many patent applications in such varied areas would be unusual and might give us more attention than wanted at the moment.

Before the toy manufacturer arrived, Barbara disclosed how she had manipulated the state records both here and in various countries she deemed appropriate for each girl, so we had "legitimate" adoption papers on each one. Somehow the waiting period had been back dated as had the documents with fake parentage and loss for each. Immigration issues had also been "smoothed over". I was just left wondering how I was going to resolve that with filing my taxes this year claiming child exemptions.

CHAPTER 13

BLACK HOLE

"Lieutenant Sapn, bring me my glasses and a cup of hot clauw," demanded General Ibn. The report of the anomaly leaving planet Aarumw was not really concerning. It had been a very small item, but the failure, again of the Klachnic to fill their fuel quota and the Orena to fill the grain coffers, or the Cowrene to provide the meat stores for the fleet were not going to go unpunished. Sipping his drink General Ibn said, "I want Prime Minister Loric, Supreme Council Leader Idenda, and President Iirilic online in the next 10."

Lieutenant Sapn replied, "Yes sir." Sharply, saluted and left to make appropriate calls.

General Ibn knew the delays were created by the rebels slowing and sabotaging their supplies. These fools thought their poor starving masses worthy of the riches that bElongged to the Bihaddi.

Bihaddi compassion for slaves suffering was foolishness. The Bihaddi were the chosen, blessed by the Initiator and all others were drudges to use to spread the holy way of the Bihaddi.

The inner Bihaddi texts, which only the enlightened elite were allowed to see, spoke to the inner heart of true followers. Manipulation, lies, cheating were the tools to infiltrate the weak. Giving them freedom was the worst of sins for they would stray from the true teaching. Worship of the dark one and dark ways was the Bihaddi path. It is the black hole that in the end rules all.

"Prime Minister Loric, this is General Ibn. We have been over this before. My fleet needs come before all others. Do you hear that screaming? That is your son. Do I make myself clear!" spoke General Ibn. He could see the blood leave Loric's face on the vid.

"Supreme Council Leader Idenda, this is General Ibn. We have been over this before. My fleet needs come before all others. Do you hear that screaming? That is your daughter. Do I make myself clear!" spoke General Ibn. He could see the blood leave Idenda's face on the vid.

"President Iirilic, this is General Ibn. We have been over this before. My fleet needs come before all others. Do you hear that screaming? That is your wife. Do I make myself clear!" spoke General Ibn. He could see the blood leave Iirilic's face on the vid.

CHAPTER 14

OVERLOAD

I was up in the north pasture clearing some invasive cedar. Hermosa ran up to me as I was putting down the chainsaw. Hermosa cried, "Come, help, something is wrong with Barbara." "Okay" I said, "Jump in the Polaris, let's get back to the house." I put the chainsaw in the back. At the house we found Barbara in her room clearly distraught with Zoe holding her right hand and Hermosa her left. She was sitting on her bed with the pink heart covers. Barbara was shaking and her lips were trembling. Deborah had gone into town taking a stallion breeding dose of semen to FedEx for overnight shipment.

I put my hand on Barbara's forehead to check for fever. Okay, no fever, but my hand was tingling, and I started getting this mad rush of information streaming across my visual plane. Inside of that I could feel Barbara screaming and crying with an intense headache. My sense was that she was overloaded, scared, and just could not take any more. She was at a breakdown point. All the girls were crying now.

Have you ever been in a room of crying women in a crisis? Not fun. Steadying myself and stepping back I said, "Give me a minute I will be right back. "Then I said, "Hermosa, come with me you need to learn this."

Being a tad over 60, Deborah and I had noticed we did not remember things like we used to. They say the brain shrinks as you age. Working with horses one learns quickly how incredibly fast they can react. There is a joke among horse people about how scary a bit of wind can make flapping feed bag to a horse. That is not a joke when in an instant that horse you were leading jumps on top of you because of something new it noticed in its environment. That is a good defense mechanism for the horse to survive in the wild, but it can be deadly to you.

Deborah and I had read where Elong Musle was doing micro dosing.

We did not know what that meant at first, but Deborah is a gifted researcher and once on the search she continues building an information base. Micro dosing is the use of minute amounts of psilocybin taken to help with mental clarity and awareness. Further researching Deborah found that periodic heroic dosing (taking grams instead of minute amounts) with psilocybin was shown to actually grow neurons in the brain and was showing great promise in overcoming addiction and Alzheimer's disease. Also, when properly monitored there seemed to be no lasting adverse side effects. There was quite a bit of information available if one was willing to find it. It was illegal to buy but buying spores for research was not. We simply grew our own for our own use only and responsibly used it to maintain mental clarity and function. Research was proving it to be very valuable for treating PTSD. Deborah and I had found it helped with mental clarity and we could remember things better. We had no desire to use it to be high.

Hermosa and I went to the closet of the master bedroom. There, Deborah had created a grow room and processing area for our mushrooms. Hermosa was fascinated now with our little mycology introduction and watched as I prepared a large dose for Barbara. The flavor is a bit earthy and not pleasant to many. I never would have considered dosing a child regularly, but I considered this an emergency situation for Barbara. The girls and I would monitor her during the process. Putting the dose in ginger tea with lemon we went back to Barbara.

I had been processing a bit of the data flow I had gotten on palming Barbara's forehead previously and felt it best to try to communicate with her via that rather than verbally to get her to drink the dose. Again, I put my hand on her forehead. Again, the tingling. Again, the data streaming. I spoke to Zoe, "Please go disconnect the fiber router power now." Zoe got up and did so. Keeping my hand on Barbara's forehead I felt the flow slow tremendously. Barbara did a big sigh and was about to lie down, but I told her to drink the dose first. She was now able to do so.

I stayed with Barbara and directed Hermosa, and Zoe to do the chores of the day. Keeping them busy would have them worry less. Deborah would be back in about two hours after getting groceries. It takes her a while to get around WalMart even with Alana helping her.

I held Barbara's hand as she laid in her bed breathing deeply. She could talk now but did not need to. The process continued and we shared communication through her neural network. She knew I was there and was comforted by my presence. I had had Zoe put on some meditative binaural music for atmosphere and further comfort. I told

Hermosa and Zoe to wait until Deborah and Alana got back to tell them as Deborah would over worry and there was no crisis now, besides I knew Deborah would be very upset with me for dosing Barbara until she fully understood.

When Deborah and Alana got back the girls were all aflutter explaining what had happened and what I was doing with Barbara. I could hear them talking as they came in with the groceries. Deborah came in eyes wide with worry and anger at me. Taking a deep calming breath I said, "Hon, please sit down and let me tell you why." With a bit of a humph she sat down, and I told her what I had seen and why I gave Barbara the dose. Barbara was very calm now, breathing deeply, and deep in her process. Deborah did not fully understand the neural data transfer. Heck, I did not either. I just had experienced it and was continuing to as I held Barbara's hand now.

CHAPTER 15

AFTER-EFFECTS

The effects were only 6 hours and then she slept, sweet, and sound. It was I who was up all night. Going over what this little gal had gone through in her short life, even with my 66 years of experience and wisdom it angered and excited me. I was amazed at what the girls had accomplished and understanding the danger our own world and lives were in. Having more knowledge of tactics and male instincts to understand the strategies of such as General Ibn. I too knew now that he was coming soon and that the girls had been trying to come up with a plan to counter the invasion. Barbara had been monitoring the media platforms and certain high government officials when the data overload became too much for her.

The next day I sat down with all four girls stating

I now understood more fully and would help them and direct them in creating a way to overcome the Bihaddi offensive. Barbara sighed deeply and I could see a relaxing of her shoulders and jaw I had not seen before. I had noticed some changes in the barn. Their vehicle was no longer visible. The skid steer and tractor were running much better, quieter, and seemed to hardly use any fuel. I knew their vehicle had utilized an antigravity system for takeoff now.

Brainstorming with the girls in the barn to be away from Alexa or other internet listening systems, I laid out requirements we would need. Our systems would need to be undetectable by authorities on the farm. They would need to be small, highly maneuverable, and weaponized, and have localized targeting. Preferably there would be multiple weapons systems, cloaking, and possibly shielding. Interface with all of the above should be intuitive and intersystem communication localized only. The Bihaddi usually came in with a fleet of three large heavy cruisers and five smaller frigates and a few destroyers. Cruisers would be carrying 5 to 10,000 troops for mop up operations after the 750 per frigate shock troops had done the initial assault. They counted on their superior computerized focused force laser systems both ship size and troop weapon sized.

They were fully capable to identifying and taking

out nuclear and rocket powered weapons based on heat signature. Their usual mode of invasion was to have infiltrated the governmental power base and media prior to invasion. That way they could inject their operatives into power by taking out the opposition and propagandize the population into submission. This was targeted to the most powerful country first and then most other countries would capitulate as it became clear opposition was futile.

We would need more money and specific supplies to upgrade the skid steer implements to weapons status. More patents were filed in my name. One was a nano sized neural link system from Barbara, which just so happened to be sent to Elong Musle right after the filing. Alana had a micro vibrating system for welding metal. The money went in the bank. The tractor barn was expanded. Changes began taking place in the skid steer and implements. Now would there be time to get everything ready.

CHAPTER 16

SQUARE DEAL

A ranch to run, holding Barbara's hand and assisting her calming the internal dialogue and processing for clues of the invasion status and collusion of involved parties were now my priorities. Not in that order though. My fun life! Just as I am focused facing a great challenge, the universe throws in the wall to climb over just to begin the solution. Something with my astrology says Deborah, something about squares. Well, if you know astrology you should know I am more of an astronomy type of guy.

First a meth head from down the road destroys his car and my fencing and then disappears. The tow truck company tells me I will pay the charges if they come out. The skid steer is out of commission while being worked on at the moment, so I pull the damn thing into the shoulder of the road with the tractor. Only a few precious hours to do that getting fencing freed and the car out of the mud hole it was stuck in. The meth head would probably come back in the middle of the night and retrieve it. So, I hoped. Otherwise, the county would have to take care of it. I could call in a fencing crew for repairs now that we had a little money to work with, but I had seen the job done by some of these crews. Again meth. How could I expect good work when their brains were fried?

With the skid steer out my main fencing equipment was too. Alana would have been a big help, but she was needed working with Zoe and Barbara. Lovely hand work for me. First, I had to put up hot wire to keep the animals in the pasture. Then I loaded the materials needed into the truck bed. Then the fun of digging 15 three-foot holes by hand with a post hole digger in Oklahoma red clay. They say chopping wood for an hour increases testosterone. After four posts I did not feel sexy just sore, tired, and my shoulder hurt and more fun to look to do the next day.

CHAPTER 17

STATUS REPORT

When I came in each evening Barbara, and I would go out to the barn shop away from the router and prying electronics. I would hold her hand and we would sift through the some of the data of the day. She had developed a filtering system now and learned to quiet the internal dialogue. She had seen how to do that from her mushroom experience and my connection. There was starting to be an uptick in emails and messaging between those we now could see were in collusion with the Bihaddi. Some of it was encrypted beyond our ability to decipher but there was enough to know their arrival would be soon.

The anti-gravitation systems were now in place on the equipment and each piece had a smart connection as well as direct wiring to the control systems in the skid steer. Life support was in place in the skid steer and forcefield systems were almost finished. The post hole digger needed a bigger hydraulic pump and heater for the cold of space. The post pounder was ready. The bale spike, forks, and bucket with teeth were ready. The laser system in the skid steer was a bit of an energy hog and would have to be used sparingly. Kinetic micro-bomb "cannons" were balanced to fire from both sides so as not to send the skid steer into a total spin. Foot pedal and hand controls were integrated with voice control and neural integration. Camera and live feed would be sent back to home base (the ranch) and via orbital satellites to be fed through the media systems overriding their server controls. Barbara was looking into communications systems as it was known the Bihaddi fed their invasion victories back to the worlds they controlled. This helped them keep the locals subservient.

We just needed a little more time.

CHAPTER 18

BIHADDI ON THE HORIZON

The Bihaddi like to come into a system from the solar opposite side to the planet they are invading. That way each ship can make the jump into an open space that has been cleared by the previous ship. This takes some time especially with so many ships and communication traffic between ships is masked by the sun. Once the whole fleet is in formation, they "steam" to the victim planet. Upon arrival they go into orbit and lock into the local communications system to present their offer of salvation to this lesser cultured world. With infiltration into the highest levels and prior propaganda systems in place this had worked marvelously well in the past. Some worlds had even capitulated without even trying to fight. There were always suckers for the local currency who willingly did the

Bihaddi bidding. Some even integrated the programming and became fanatics for the cause prior to invasion.

General Ibn had been working on this world for a few years. Some 30 years ago this planet orbiting in the habitable zone had been located. Small monitoring devices had been sent at first. With indications of intelligent life small infiltrating units had been sent. Volunteers for these missions were numerous as they were given great autonomy and could feed their dark desires wantonly on the locals. There are no ethical limits to the Bihaddi with these lesser creatures. Desire, money, power these were the tools of missionaries.

With our fleet now rounding the sun we were salivating for the rape of this new world as it came under Bihaddi domination.

CHAPTER 19

GREETING PARTY

Telescopic anomaly reporting was our first indication. It was first one, then numerous. The press first reported a meteor constellation rounding the sun. We suspected different. As resolution and trajectory came into better focus there was first fear then curiosity and then fear in the media. In our hearts there was resolve.

Barbara now knew that I was the one to take our little greeting party to the Bihaddi fleet. I now knew as well as she the Bihaddi ships and their tactics. Each girl was just too valuable, yes even my wife. I made my necessary changes in my Last Will and Testament giving all the royalties from patents to the appropriate girl. I knew my equipment with each upgrade and had strategies in mind for each. The Bihaddi liked to come in the morning side of a planet flaunting their superiority. I would be stationed in orbit fully cloaked looking like space junk in a cluster. My takeoff would be fully cloaked, no rockets flashing just anti-grav and minor gyroscopic adjustments.

I loaded my old 9 mm and added a few clips to my chest pocket. That would be a last resort if shielding went down as each bullet would send me careening in the opposite direction. Kisses and hugs from each girl and tears from my wife and I boarded my little craft. I almost got a fly by from one of the fighter jets out of the Airforce base but shifted direction and accelerated altitude before he came close. Slipping into my high altitude orbit I stayed quiet and dark monitoring the Bihaddi approach.

CHAPTER 20

GENERAL IBN AND ADMIRAL ARYG

General Ibn had risen from a street urchin, without family or friend. He had been taken in by the Supreme Initiator and raised in his household. The men under his command knew him as stern but fair in the Bihaddi way. The rules were clear. Follow the commands from above in detail. Pay due respect to your officers. No looting or raping until all was secure and always keep a guard of two men when the others in your squad were canvassing the local area for prize.

Admiral Aryg's was from a long naval tradition going back to ocean vessels. Now with mastery of his fleet and having good rapport with his captains and his history of many victories working with General Ibn in troop and equipment transport and enemy stronghold softening he felt confident in this local invasion. There seemed to be but token resistance so far with just a few missiles launched from below. Destroying them early in their flight was easy with their primitive technology. General Ibn would be simply mopping up resistance after he softened each major governing capital. Confidence was high with all of his officers.

General Ibn was on deck with Admiral Aryg monitoring the fleet approach and local resistance. Monitoring the local media systems which indicated these people were already demoralized. Already the prerecorded Bihaddi offer of taking over to advance their world civilization was broadcasting. This would be another soft take over. Realtime burst transfers of video and audio back to Bihaddi space of the invasion progress had been started with the first takeover offer.

Moral among the troops was high as they watched the monitors on their face shields. Most were crack troops from previous invasions but there were a few new recruits sewn in to follow the seasoned ones. All were well trained, and each knew his duty. There was to be no mercy to resistance and protection of valued women and prized possessions.

CHAPTER 21

STEALTH APPROACH

My instruments gave me a display of the Bihaddi fleet. I counted six destroyers, three frigates, and three heavy cruisers. Having knowledge of each of the ship designs from Barbara, I could tell they were all facing away from my little unit. I had strongly suspected the Bihaddi would be focused on their goal and my approach might not be monitored closely. Each of my implements had intelligent preprogramming as to target ship systems. The bale spike had been converted to deliver micro-bot bombs that would seek out and destroy power source and battery backup for each Destroyer. It was designed to pierce, deliver its payload, extract itself, and move to the next one. I hoped this micro-bot insertion bale spike would be misinterpreted as a minor piece of space junk collision and be basically ignored as the bale spike continued to do its job among the destroyers. I released the bale spike first as the destroyers were the most likely to detect me and put my little flotilla in danger. Also, once in action I hoped this would create some chaos among the fleet.

The skid steer forks, and post pounder were sent to take out the frigates. The forks would deliver nanotech spores into the life support system in each frigate. These would incapacitate the nervous systems while the post pounder would attach to the hull and drive the communications antenna into their bridge control panel. Again, these were designed to work quickly, in tandem, and move onto the next frigate, preferably before warning could be sent to rest of the fleet.

The cruisers were a bigger deal. I was already headed into the rear cruiser and detection might happen soon. My bucket had been lined with special surfacing and would act as a shield reflecting back any laser fire directed at me. It remained attached to the skid steer. I had sent the auger to the forward cruiser a few seconds after sending the other implements to the frigates. The auger was designed to drive through the center of the ship down into the life support systems and on into the power system. That left me with the skid steer with its kinetic micro cannons and my bucket.

I was maneuvering to be in position between the rear and mid cruiser. With any luck they would fire on me and hit the bucket reflector and have it redirected back to them. If they missed, they might hit the mid cruiser. My size relative to them was smaller than a buffalo gnat on a buffalo. If they did not know I was there by now they were searching for me. I was seeing energy signatures shutting down on the destroyers and frigates now. Communication traffic was now coming in heavy from the forward cruiser. Spaceships need to be light but structurally strong. Heavy steel is well, heavy and strong. That auger was ripping through that cruiser on its destructive mission and all they could do was watch as it bore through deck after deck. The cruiser weapons were outward directed not inward. They might be able to hit it with hand weapons, but it was moving fast and throwing shrapnel with no gravity to slow those piercing particles.

Uh oh. Though I remained directly between the mid and rear cruiser the rear cruiser had gotten a lock on my little ship. My bucket shield was untested, and I was only a kilometer from their lasers. There was no real distanced to dissipate the power of their weapons. Also, their energy weapons would act like a hammer hitting a nail. All my energy shielding would have to be to my rear as I crashed into the mid cruiser. The girls and I were counting on this.

CHAPTER 22

SWATTING THE BUFFALO GNAT

Admiral Aryg thought, "With all ships in appropriate approach position and spirits high both naval and invasion force this should be a routine mission." Sitting comfortably in his command chair he was monitoring the data feed coming from his other ships and the reports as his ship commanders maneuvered compensating for gravity pulls and using the usual laser vaporization of space junk that had already accumulated around this planet. The little laser flashes were reassuring. His job was the fleet. That is what he loved. The orchestration was like a symphony conductor directing men and machines.

General Ibn liked to walk through the bulkheads where his men were stationed during a planetary approach. He maintained full video visibility and feedback with the other officers on the other ships where the men could watch video of his progress comforting and encouraging them as they prepared for their tasks.

Orientation in space must be three dimensional from a reference point. This had been established as best from the command cruiser. Destroyers had been oriented at 30 degrees centered on the front cruiser in a 5-kilometer radius. The frigates behind them centered on the command mid cruiser.

When the first destroyers had gone dark it was thought a malfunction or stray piece of space junk must have caused some communications damage. Standard operating procedure was implemented, and all channel micro laser light signals were aimed to the dark ship. Then as another ship went dark and then another Admiral Aryg put the fleet on full alert. All sensors were put on full feed through the computer systems and communication and sensor officers were scanning the environs. Something was happening. Admiral Aryg and General Ibn knew outward calm was essential to keep their men focused. This type of resistance had not been seen before. It had to be something in the local system, probably some kind of radiation effect from the local sun. Proper communication screening should take care of this.

When the first frigate sent in a partial message of distress and then went dark General Ibn cut the current feed to the troops and looped in feed from the previous invasion process. Some might notice the inconsistency but not all.

Admiral Aryg took calming breaths, calmed his voice, and addressed his captains, "We are the Bihaddi. We are professionals. The god of our fathers will give us victory. Stay your course. Stay in touch. Use your sensors. Use your senses. Captains use your discretion wisely."

It was at this time that the rear cruiser got a lock on my energy signature realizing my little ship was more that a piece of space junk.

"Narrow focus main laser, 1.2-degree arc," commanded Captain Reeng of the rear cruiser. He was going to have his laser vaporize through the center of this interloper cutting it in half. It would be a sweep but would focus only on that damn craft with no overflow.

The firing officer reported, "Coordinates locked on, arc set, fire ready."

Captain Reeng gave his command, "Fire."

The full force of the rear cruiser's own laser power sliced through the center of rear cruiser splitting all the men in the command center, severing all the control panels, cutting through into the center of the ship destroying the main gyroscopic controls and breaching the power center. Without power, with air jetting out of the front of the cruiser it began to decelerate and reverse. Breech sirens were sounding in the bays that still had air. Those where vacuum was rapidly stealing breath were in chaos as men and machine struggled to close the sliced gap and save what hope of life was left. All bays were sealed in accordance with well-practiced routines. They were now adrift out of earth orbit caught by the moon's gravitation. The few escape pods were only designed to hold officers and staff. There was no access for the grunts. Passageways were locked. Backup power would give them a few days off air circulation and limited lighting. Different bays could communicate with one another, and the video show of the current battle continued to flow to the Bihaddi planets.

CHAPTER 23

INVASION OF THE BUFFALO GNAT

Alana with Hermosa had developed a Gel foam encasing system that wrapped around me absorbing that shock as the full energy of the laser beam hit my reflecting bucket. That it was just a fraction of a second did not change the opposite and equal reaction of my vessel to that energy charge. The reflective mirror system worked wonderfully but there was plenty of power left over to superheat my bucket and push me rapidly into the mid cruiser. Thank God there was an ablative surface underneath the mirroring. None the less the heat transfer through bucket attachments was now burning through the soles of my feet. The rubber soles of my boots melted. There was no time for reaction on my part as my skid steer went slamming through the hull of the mid cruiser and on through the hull, and through the rear troop bay, pushing men and equipment into the center of the ship crushing all. Without the Gel foam packing I was in I would have been reduced to jam in a jar.

As it was, in order for me to survive Hermosa had programmed her survival systems to load me with anti-inflammatories and put my body in a coma. It was only later that I would get to watch the occurrences of the next hour. On autopilot once my momentum had been absorbed by the cruiser my shielding went to full 360 mode. Then my kinetic cannons began their firing sequence after maneuvering out of the cruiser. They cut a circle around the command center followed by multiple diameters of that circle. At the same time the kinetic force was pushing the skid steer away from the Bihaddi fleet. Once fully clear my lovely autopilot put on cloaking to take the skid steer back home.

CHAPTER 24

ACTIONS AND REACTIONS

Barbara, Alana, and Zoe had been busy while I was having my little vacation from the ranch. The president and vice president had been very busy with the large media companies stating how resistance was futile to this more advanced culture. The most advanced systems they had sent to intercept them had been immediately destroyed. Besides they would elevate our world to better things. The major social media platform was censoring any attempts at promoting resistance.

When the President received report of anomaly detected by the pilot when I was ascending to my rendezvous with the Bihaddi fleet and then watched the Bihaddi video of their great invasion pickup of my presence, he immediately sent a stand down order. As the disintegration of the Bihaddi fleet began appearing on their own feed into the media systems, the major outlets began shutting down their feed of the invasion claiming technical difficulties.

It was at that point that Barbara, Alana, and Zoe patched in the feed from my little craft coupled with holographic man dialogue giving the history of the Bihaddi and how they subjugated peoples, enslaving, brutalizing, and destroying. Then holographic man began displaying the evidence of collusion between those in power and the media outlets with the Bihaddi. Social media servers were shut down, but somehow, they continued to function without censorship.

Secret service agencies were ordered to do a hit on holographic man. They were searching frantically but feed into the network was not coming from one area, it was a dispersed system. They thought it might be bitcoin integrated.

As the full rout of the Bihaddi invasion fleet was displayed free peoples of the world stood astonished. Then with disclosure of treason by collusion with a foreign power by the media, social media, and governing powers there was an uproar. The president and his staff locked themselves in the Presidential Emergency Operations Center. The vice president did the same at Camp David. Those involved in treason were no longer able to hide and their cohorts hiding them in the media, FBI, and CIA were now fully outed. The speaker of the house was immediately arrested as congress went into emergency session. Similar things were happening in other countries. Orders were no longer heeded by these betrayers as the money transfers and perversions they engaged in were now exposed.

CHAPTER 25

CATCHING BREATH

Thank goodness with all this the little vessel that returned to home was almost forgotten. The skid steer was immediately taken into the barn and my body taken out bruised with burned feet, mild brain swelling from the trauma still in a coma. The gel was washed off. My body put in a bed with intravenous fluids and DMSO to reduce brain swelling. With four girls and a loving wife I could not have gotten better care.

With damage to the skid steer from the heat and shock the cloaking systems were not quite fully functioning and on review of data from that day, the Airforce in Enid had been able to detect something returning from space in a controlled manner. It had taken a week for them to locate our general area. Woods and hills had obscured the end of descent, but it was enough for them to follow satellite data and watch the descent all the way into the barn.

Further research showed we were ranchers who raised a few horses. We paid our taxes. Nothing remarkable until patents began to be filed in the last few months. Three remarkable patents filed in the same name. It was time to pay a visit to this rancher.

CHAPTER 26
BUFFALO NICKEL

The swelling had gone down, and I was awakened. My body felt weak and bruised. My feet ached though I could not see them as they were encased in the poultice Hermosa kept on them. I was getting four meals a day now but could only eat half portions. Barbara would hold my hand for our neural connection, and I could feel her struggle to keep from crying. Mostly I slept. Deborah and Barbara decided I needed a heroic dose of Golden Teacher mushroom. They gave me mushroom laced ginger and lemon tea instead of a meal. Binaural brain healing music was put on earphones as I laid in bed for the next six hours. Barbara held my hand and watched as I went through the battle sequence processing the trauma of that laser smash and the burns I was receiving as well as the anguish of the souls dying by my hands.

The next day I awoke with more of an appetite. I wanted to go out and visit my horses but found I could still barely walk and that not without serious pain. We still had an old wheelchair from when Deborah's mother had lived with us those last months of her life. I still had my lucky buffalo nickel on the chain at my chest. The Gel foam had protected me from having that heat up. They now had me on a diet of colostrum blender drinks to provide added nutrition and growth hormone to aid healing. Arnica Montana was salved on the bruises.

It was a few days later, I was out on the front porch listening to the birds and enjoying a light breeze when the dogs started barking. Then I heard the clunk, clunk of someone driving over the bridge covering the creek feeding into our property, then another clunk clunk and another. The paired close succession indicated three vehicles. This was an unusual occurrence in our little valley. Then across the pasture I saw three new black Humvee cars going to our drive and turning in. The girls and Deborah were on alert now as well as all the dogs barking. The girls and Deborah were all ready to take my inside. I said no. I was back to being fully cognizant and told them to go inside.

This would be between me and them. No one knew of the girl's involvement. Few knew of their presence. Any responsibility needed to fall on me and keep them free.

I am not a military person. I recognized those getting out of the vehicles to be in full dress uniform though. As they approached the gate, I greeted them saying, "How may I help you gentlemen?"

The one with the star on his shoulders answered, "My name is Brigadier General Adams. We would like to ask you a few questions about some recent occurrences that seem to be related to this location."

"Sure," I said. "I am Bill. You are welcome to have a seat but there are only three chairs on my porch. Also, I apologize, I would stand but I burned my feet a little over a week ago when I was trying to put out a fire that got out of hand when wind gusted as I was burning a brush pile." I noted some of the men going into the stall barn and some others walking around to the hay barn/tool barn. I hope the girls had put the tires back on the skid steer and touched up the paint to hide the burns.

Deborah came out and asked, "Iced tea, gentleman, or I have some coffee made if you prefer?" There were polite denials, but I did notice some takers of the fresh baked German chocolate cake that was offered and some taking a chocolate chip pecan cookie. Deborah set the food tray down and went back in the house. The girls, though hidden, I suspected were watching closely.

Brigadier General Adams then said, "We noted an anomaly on our radar scanner record from ten days ago that seemed to come to this location. This was right after the alien invasion that was intercepted. Have you or anyone here seen or heard anything you could share with us?"

I answered and pointed, "We have had some UFO activity in this area. My wife and I saw one hover over our front pasture about 100 yards out there a few years past."

It was then a young first lieutenant came up to the porch from the direction of the tool barn where the skid steer was parked. He was smiling and first saluted his general, awaiting response. Brigadier General Adams nodded and simply commanded, "Report."

The first lieutenant said as he toyed with the pen in his shirt pocket, "There is a skid steer in the barn. The controls are different from any I have seen. There is burn under the paint and there are no skid steer implements in the area. None on the farm as far as I can tell. Then with a wicked grin he swiftly pulled the pen from his pocket and fired a pinpoint laser right at the center of my chest. I grimaced as my lucky buffalo nickel went white hot on my chest and the silver alloy chain melted dropping the nickel on the porch. He was in the midst of a Bihaddi war cry as Barbara blasted through his head with my old 9 mm right through the master bedroom window.

I do not curse often but said, "Damn now I know how a horse feels when it is branded." Four girls had tumbled out on the porch surrounding me, Barbara still brandishing my old pistol.

Brigadier General Adams commanded his men, "Stand down."

I gently took the gun from Barbara saying, "Its okay now girls I am fine. If he had a partner, they would have worked in tandem and then I would be hurt."

Deborah at that point demanded, "Bill take your shirt off I have to see that wound."

I rolled my eyes and unbuttoned. There on my sternum was the perfect imprint of a buffalo nickel complete with imprint of the buffalo. It was also really starting to hurt, and I flinched as she touched it. Deborah commanded Hermosa, "Get some ice and aloe vera."

CHAPTER 27

INTRODUCTIONS AND EXPLANATIONS

Brigadier General Adams was smiling now, "Would you please introduce me to your family?"

In reply I shared, "General Adams, I hope you are a reasonable man with family and are willing to listen and understand. Let me introduce my adopted daughters from the planet Aarumw, which was recently captured by the Bihaddi. I am certain you have reviewed the video feed of both the Bihaddi and our own as I intervened. They are the architects of this Bihaddi defeat and I just an old rancher who could not let his family suffer coming under their abuse. "

Thus, as Brigadier General Adams and his men listened now sipping iced tea as the sun continued to warm and my girls served cookies and topped off tea, the story of these incredible girls was shared. Of course, there were a few corrections to my ramblings by each girl as I tried to relate technical aspects of their work or explain the workings of the world and cultures they came from.

Finally, Deborah intervened as weariness began to sit heavy on my shoulders and head. It was then I asked, "Brigadier General Adams I ask you and your men please do not report the presence of my girls? I know the Bihaddi will continue to hunt me for their revenge. Do not put these fine women in the sights of their vengeance."

Brigadier General Adams looked at his men and the body of the fallen Bihaddi and assured me this would be done. He too had seen the levels of corruption by those in positions of power that had been exposed. He too was certain there were more infiltrators who would seek knowledge of the agent of their defeat. He too had a wife and children he loved as did each man there. With that I was wheeled into my house and slept.

CHAPTER 28

GIMPING INTO THE FUTURE

I was healing nicely. My feet were not as painful, but they remained tender. I noted some new nicer looking younger men driving into the junker place of my neighbor. Their vehicles were newer and had mufflers that worked. Our world was changing. Traitors and betrayers were now being exposed, arrested, and brought to trial, this even at the highest level of government, business, and society. Status, money, and media propaganda no longer protected them.

The girls were now going to high school and taking college courses. They loved the social interaction and remained fiercely loyal to one another. Woe to any boy or girl who crossed this group. They rose early in the morning, got the chores done, ate, and went to school during the weekdays. Horses were the passion in the evenings. Horse talk with Deborah was the bulk of dinner conversation. I noticed some of the young men who now lived as our neighbors had an appreciation of the livestock and would watch as the girls rode in the arena. Of course, the girls were aware of this attention and glowed, giggling at times with each other about a handsome young man hanging on the arena straps as they practiced dressage or jumping. Deborah was their mentor, a full time and fulfilling life for her.

Holographic man was whom the girls had imposed on all the vid feed that went out during the battle. It was fully hoped that he would be whom all would seek to find. A fitting persona as he was the representation of Barbara's father, whom she would probably never see again. The old skid steer never quite worked right again. We bought new Quick Attach implements and a bigger skid steer. Money was coming in on royalties from the patents filed by the girls in my name. I would go out to do a chore, repair a bit of fence or milk the cow and find the girls had already done it.

It was at this point I wondered what effect sending holographic man as a robot with a skid steer and implements would have on the Bihaddi when it appeared back at the captured worlds.

The girls were excited about this believing it

would help the rebel movement. I had kept in touch with Brigadier General Adams via his men next door. He came out to visit and I suggested he have some men help in the construction and process to better understand the technology. It was great to have purpose again and I did not have to be on my feet too much.

CHAPTER 29

WHERE ARE YOU GOING?

Barbara had done a rapid set of patent filing and internet wide dump of the anti-gravitational and other technologies the girls had developed as soon as the Bihaddi defeat became apparent. This was at my request so these could not be restricted by government intervention. She had also included direct communication with Elong Musle about using his Star Link system for suppression of com link bursts by Bihaddi operatives still working on the planet.

Surprise had been the biggest factor in our victory. The skid steer had been a convenient device. It was not the best design for further struggles except as propaganda. It was strongly suspected the Bihaddi had become lax and arrogant with their many past victories. With some luck the full vid of our battle would have been widely viewed by those in the captured worlds as the Bihaddi had done in the past, touting their greatness. I strongly suspected the vid records would be studied closely and their generals would be creating strategies to defeat us in the future.

The ships still orbiting our planet were a huge danger and potential asset. They might not be speeding meteors causing destruction but still were large enough to be dangerous. Besides retrofitting and repair of their ships gave us technology and needed fire power. From infrared readings there were pockets of surviving soldiers in some of the ships. Their capture and interrogation might prove useful. Interpretation would either have to be done by one of the girls or a duplicated Holographic man.

The girls had now shared with Brigadier General Adams, who was our designated liaison, the designs and battle plans they had of the Bihaddi. The anti-gravitational systems were rapidly studied and incorporated by Space X.

Tinker Airforce Base in Oklahoma City was now the center for manufacturing anti-gravitational drives to retrofit the Bihaddi ships before their orbits decayed too much. There had already been two

Destroyers that had their orbits decay and had mostly burned up with debris careening into the Pacific Ocean. Fortunately. none were hurt but this might not be the case in the future. Recovery ships were sent to retrieve what they could.

After neural link connection and being around the girls talking so much I was becoming fluent in their native language. Sometimes I would slip into it without even being aware when talking with them. If someone else was around I might notice a puzzled look on their face and make the change back to English.

There was some talk by certain "classified" individuals in positions of power about confining the girls to an alien research facility for further study. Barbara first detected this via her neural link monitoring and some connections she established with Anonymous, a decentralized international activist and hacktivist collective and movement. Using the girl's language, I told her to keep any connections with Anonymous very well guarded and private. The government might become suspicious of you if they knew of them which could lead to problems. She was livid, as were Alana, Hermosa, and Zoe when they heard of this.

"Girls," I explained in their language, "There are

those when training horses think a heavy, controlling, confining hand gets them quick results with the behavior they want. This works in the sense that they see responses they want. What they do not see is the potential of the animal. They do not see the joy they could share with the animal. A gentle, patient, loving guiding and teaching hand makes the horse your partner. The horse wants to perform and do the things that come naturally to him for your praise. He is a herd animal used to the rub and grooming affection of his fellows. He recognizes and respects the herd leader. Have each of you seen how a baby horse will do baby chomps with his mouth telling an older horse please be kind I am younger and recognize you as higher in herd hierarchy?"

Alana was the first who said, "Yes." Then Zoe, Hermosa, and Barbara nodded in agreement.

I continued, "We too are herd animals. We are designed for love. Love as agape. That means compassion and caring from our fellows. Regrettably we must deal with those who act like a rank stallion thinking they can control us and get what they want by biting and kicking the mares. They think they are top of the hierarchy and have no accountability for their actions. How do you think the mares respond when given a choice between the rank stallion and one who sweet talks them and nuzzles them and tells them in his horse fashion he cares?"

Hermosa said, "The mares always want to go to the nice stallion."

"So," I said, "We have a potential problem with certain people who think we are just horses in their herd to control. They cannot or do not see us as the individuals and persons we are and value us properly. You experienced this with the Bihaddi. What did you do to change that?"

Barbara answered, "I started monitoring information, learning, and getting friends to help me escape."

"Good." I said.

Alana said, "I studied the engineering of the Bihaddi and began working on our ships plans."

"Good." I said.

Hermosa responded, "I studied my plants and means to have food and air and what we needed for our ship."

"Good. I continued.

Zoe shared, "I made robots to help us."

"Let us see. You acquired allies in you endeavor. You created a plan to respond. You worked together each within their respective talents. You carried out your plan created a ship and fled the Bihaddi."

In unison the girls said, "Yes we did."

"It is time for us to do these things here but with a

twist. We make a plan. We work together. We acquire allies. This time though, we do not flee. We fight. We prepare our plan for the Bihaddi and for those who would enslave us here. This time we do not just flee. We prepare a fight plan, equipment, and system."

CHAPTER 30

INTERNAL PREPARATIONS

The natural tendency for many people in a system is to protect their position. We see this in our government all too often. Bureaucrats and others in positions of power have their own personal agendas. I explained to the girls, "Trusting others to know or even want what you need can be dangerous to you. We know there are others aligned with the Bihaddi in this world. Also, sometimes people in positions of power have other ideas and alliances that run against ours. You need to use your resources, allies, friends, research abilities to not only know all who can influence your life and plans but to know their weaknesses. As you did with the invasion, use those weaknesses to keep your freedom."

It was then I asked each of the girls, "What is it

that is different from being here than your home world? What is it you love about being here?"

Their answer was said in unison, "Our freedom."

I questioned, "But why freedom? You were fed. You had shelter. You were to be wed, have children."

Then as Barbara held her friend's hands completing their quick neural link after a minute's thought she answered, "We had those things, but they were bitter. We were fed and housed. We were to be wed but not to our choosing. We were owned and owned nothing not even ourselves. Without freedom we had nothing. That we had food, clothing, and shelter was for another's convenience that we had value for them. Our lives and everything we did was to increase the wealth of others. We were to be kept as long as we had value to them. The heart of my being, or each of us rebelled against this. My value is not in the accounts of another's ledger. My value resides in the infinite spark within my heart. My freedom allows me the opportunity to learn this life's lessons. I am more than this body, more than this brain. I am a soul on a journey."

"Excellent." I said, "Then you have the base to understand the struggle I will outline. The Bihaddi would enslave us all if they are able. They are not the only ones who seek to do this though. In this world you have come to there is a long history of those who would set themselves up as above accountability, those who by wealth, power, or position would have separated themselves from consequences to their abusive actions and manipulations. They consider themselves better than the lesser peoples. We are the deplorables. They game the systems to their advantage and punish all who would threaten their domination."

Barbara answered for the girls, "Oh."

I continued, "I tell you this so you understand the seemingly stupid resistance you will experience to deal with the Bihaddi. These elitists may see some of the things you are working on as a threat to their power, their plans. If we can understand them as our enemy as well and understand their thinking, we have a better chance of defeating the Bihaddi and bettering the world you are now in."

CHAPTER 31

WISE AS SERPENTS—GENTLE AS DOVES

Following a chain of command from the known persons to those whom they answer to can get some interesting results. There is an old saying, follow the money. That leads to those not listed in that chain of command. Often these are the real persons wielding power. Knowing we were being monitored for our internet accesses and contacts, we had to rely on more surreptitious means of research. I was working with Barbara, via our hand-held neural link connection. She was researching WikiLeaks and working with Anonymous and other resources researching money flow and influence and donations from various sources without leaving an internet IP address via her internal linkage. The command structure of money flow and influence linked certain influential persons in our Representatives, Senators, and the Executive branch of our government as well as highly placed bureaucrats who yielded a pattern of betrayal and undermining of our Constitutional experiment. There seemed to be no accountability by these persons for the fact that they had sworn to uphold and defend the Constitutional contract and their repeated efforts to tear down that very contract.

Enemies are those who have forgotten we are all connected. Enemies are those who think they gain or maintain by causing suffering. I wished to be enemies to none. I felt myself an enemy to none but fully effused with paternal protection for those close to me and for my world. This was not a game. I am here and I am fully engaged. I am engaged not in anger but in the love of life. I am the agent of life giving accountability to those who have separated themselves from compassion. I am fierce and unafraid. I am swift and deadly. I am the ultimate love they have never seen.

Thus, while viewing enemies in our world and enemies in the Bihaddi worlds we created weapons. Weapons of disclosure, connections, money flow, and treason exposure of enemies in our world and weapons of destruction and demoralization and exposure in the Bihaddi worlds. I am the hammer of reality to awaken those dulled in the sleep of their delusion and fanaticism. I am relentless.

There was much on the news about the Bihaddi ships finally being stabilized in orbit after incredible amounts of effort and cooperation among many nations. There was a global sigh of relief that that immediate danger was averted. The ship that crashed into the moon created a dust cloud that put a temporary dust atmosphere about the moon obscuring close observation.

General Ibn had managed to get to his escape pod and thus had atmosphere for breath and supplies for a short duration. Lieutenant Sapn had come with him but he had suffered severe injuries from shrapnel. General Ibn had managed to staunch his bleeding, but internal injuries were beyond his medical acumen. Lieutenant Sapn's body had had to be jettisoned as it would start rotting and foul the limited air of the pod. The pod had been released shortly after the battle with care to stay on the moon side of the ship to avoid planetary detection. A small observation base had been set up on the dark side of the moon. There was a small ship there he could requisition for his return to Bihaddi headquarters. He was already working out his plans for revenge. The whole damn planet would suffer his heavy hand when he returned with the full fleet. There would be no such surprise occurring again upon his return.

CHAPTER 32

WAR OF DISTRACTION

What had been a surprise the first time was not going to surprise again. We needed new tactics and engineering. Having greater resources was a great boon. Having bureaucracy to work with was a drag. With a coming battle imminent appearing to be fully cooperative with the Brigadier General Adams and his associates as well as the other branches of military and government was in our best interests. Deborah is more politically correct than I as I can be a bit abrupt. After all who can resist a sweet gray-haired blue-eyed lady who comes with cookies, listens politely, talks nicely, and totally pegs you to the wall. There was no way she was going to allow anyone to take advantage of her girls. Having our neural link dark web hacktivist backup provided a great resource for having the background to get around the many blocks that were thrown our way. We made it very clear that no one got near the girls except through Deborah and I.

Some little scuttle butt about my skid steer was suspected by the paparazzi but the military put out distractions and disinformation about a craft coming down in Canada or New Mexico after the battle. The picture anonymously leaked was a mini space shuttle. Somehow mockups of these with burn marks appeared in Alberta and near Santa Rosa. These of course were seized immediately upon discovery by the military for "national security reasons". Thus, no close inspections. A partially burned body was found a few hundred yards from the Santa Rosa Shuttle. It was the body of the Bihaddi spy Barbara had shot. Of course, no DNA matches could be found for him or even familial matches. Thus, speculation grew that he was an alien hero who had saved us. Great expense was made by the media to recreate his facial features from the burned body. The politicians dove into the process. Votes were taken and with great pomp and media coverage he was given a hero's burial. The worlds unknown soldier buried at the United Nations.

Interestingly just before the ritual there was a terrorist bombing attempt at the mausoleum prior to the body internment. A small cadre of terrorists were captured who claimed to be Bihaddi operatives. When Barbara and the girls listened to their speech between each other and when asked questions in the Bihaddi languages there was no response. They had been recruited by some Bihaddi operatives and turned fanatic. The only ones hurt in the explosion were the idiot fanatics catching some shrapnel in their backs as they ran. The damage was minor and quickly repaired in time for the ritual internment, which of course was broadcast over the world.

Follow up on who the Bihaddi operatives were, was undertaken by the CIA and FBI and Interpol. I heard no more of what was happening with that but there was some gossip rag articles about laser battles holes burned in corporate buildings complete with pictures of burned holes through concrete and glass.

CHAPTER 33

GENERAL IBN HOMECOMING

On return to the outpost world of Aarumw general Ibn was greeted with a very different reception. The fleet he had taken to earth had reduced local forces significantly. That coupled with the full disclosure of the absolute defeat of the invading armada had triggered rebellion or rebellious sentiments across the Bihaddi captured worlds. Smaller outposts had been attacked and forces had to be concentrated for protection. Given these conditions it seemed most critical to General Ibn to immediately gather forces, develop appropriate strategies and attack with an overwhelming force to quell this rebellion and show the worlds that the Bihaddi were still invincible.

Throwing himself into crushing the rebels he allowed his revenge to smolder. It was a burn inside him that drove him. He could see clearly that no mercy could be given. All who made themselves a danger to his beloved Bihaddi, no manner the age or sex faced the sword of his anger. This was his world, his universe. Kindness was for those who worked with him. Love was for those who shared his passion. His troops received the full embrace of his heart as they felt the whip to drive them to win. This was his race with life and he would win!

CHAPTER 34

OFFENSE THE BEST DEFENSE

General Adams consulted with us often as Barbara and the girls were the asset with the most knowledge of the Bihaddi, their culture, history, and war strategies. Retro engineering of the spaceships technologies was now better understood. The girls were young women now. They had finished high school and were well into college level studies. Their studies, they found could all be done online. They loved this as it allowed them to stay with each other and the horses they had grown to love. They would ride a nice hack around the property trails several times a week together. When spring came again, they would go murel hunting as they had grown to love these fried with their breakfast. It was during a morel hunt that Barbara had the thought to defeat the Bihaddi using what they feared the most.

The Bihaddi had all seen the skid steer that had destroyed their invading fleet. Now this symbol of fear and destruction could be used as both a decoy and a delivery device of the true destructive means of their defeat. Thus, the girls established their neural link there in the quiet woods as their horses grazed just down slope in open pasture. What they did not know was the young men who had been watching them and now they had grown to love would be the first to volunteer.

Sharing the history of the Bihaddi, Barbara and the girls made clear their return in greater numbers was not a question of if but when. That they would develop different strategies was certain. Coordinates and ability to travel to their worlds were now tools we had. What strategies could we employ? Certainly, they had more infrastructure and experience with space warfare.

When the girls disclosed the sensor sweep and destruction of their discharge when they entered the solar system, there was concern about a Bihaddi base in the system. Given the Bihaddi tactics and knowledge of the solar system as well as infiltration within earth governments and military it was obvious there had been significant investment in study of the local system. Using the moon as a local base to facilitate infiltration and communications with Bihaddi home worlds would be a logical and efficient choice. Since such a base would allow relatively easy monitoring of earth-side communications an investigation of the dark side of the moon was planned.

General Adams had been promoted to head of the United States Space Force due to his more in-depth knowledge of the systems used by the Bihaddi and his work with Barbara, Hermosa, Alana, and Zoe. He was putting together a task force to find the Bihaddi moon base and had plenty of volunteers among his men but none of them had full knowledge of the Bihaddi language to read or translate if needed and to read body language to anticipate deception.

The girls had now become proficient in the martial arts and weapon usage as they knew they would be prime Bihaddi targets. The young men guarding our place and observing the girls had been quite happy to volunteer to teach the girls. During this teaching process I noticed how Zoe and her "teacher" had become quite close. He was chosen to head the expedition to the moon and thus Zoe volunteered to go.

General Adams was reluctant to send one of his best robotics engineers and micro-bot engineers but with much persuasion and consideration of possible scenarios she was deemed the best choice in the emergent situation. Barbara was was just too central to all planning. Alana was in depth reverse engineering Bihaddi ship systems working with her team. Hermosa was deep in anticancer and reversal of degenerative damage from space radiation exposure.

Master Sergeant Steven Sandhurst and Ms. Zoe began training with Space X for their secret getaway. They were both very competent having knowledge of their craft, suits, sensors, displays, etc. The ship had special cloaking non-reflective surface and communications would be minimal to none after takeoff until their objective was achieved. They worked very well together and could be a very deadly force if needed. The ruse Space X was going to feed the media was that this was an experimental flight with the booster working but the drone ship failing after orbit with proof by total failure of communications and disappearance of the ship in a mock explosion.

What these young healthy in love people did once untethered from earth on their way to the moon is, well none of my business! As they came in a low orbit around the dark side of the moon their sensors began reading telemetry from a southern polar crater. On their next pass they guided their craft to the inside edge of the crater. On landing there was a metallic ding that rang through their craft. They had already donned their suits and prepared their weapon systems on the craft. With the ding they expected resistance. To their surprise a port opened near the center of the crater. Nothing came out but there was a Bihaddi language message they heard in their earpieces begging them for food. A man named Whisper Gee introduced himself saying he had been abandoned there by the Bihaddi after General Ibn left with his escape ship. He had managed to subsist on the stores he had but he was almost totally out. He had no way to contact the planet and was getting no more messages from the Bihaddi.

Zoe, of course, translated all of this for Steven. Steven decided they would approach the port keeping 30 meters apart. Both had head cams that were now recording and would automatically jettison the full recordings to go earth-side and send their data if there was any trauma to them or on command if needed. Once in the port, they stood back-to-back in ready position as the port closed and took them down in an elevator type fashion to a holding room that had appropriate atmosphere and temperature. Then Zoe saw the poor disheveled Whisper Gee who was practically groveling he was so happy to see another person after such a long time and living without hope of survival. Zoe released her helmet and Whisper Gee was astounded to see a young woman. Steven now has his helmet off and Whisper Gee proceeded to give them a guided tour of the facility. Zoe and he carried on a rapid conversation which Steven only partly caught. Whisper Gee was telling Zoe how his tribe had been enslaved by the Bihaddi when he was prepubescent. They were in a tropical region and the Bihaddi considered them stupid and weak and only useful for menial tasks. They were also used sometimes in outposts where the Bihaddi might leave them to die of starvation or exposure. He had been brought to this outpost years before and they had provisioned him until their invasion failure. Then General Ibn had come in a damaged escape pod and requisitioned the outpost escape ship. He had felt the Bihaddi ship crash into the moon, but it was too far for him to get to and get back to his base without running out of air. Whisper Gee had known to never use the escape ship as they would immediately kill him upon return. He had seen vid of this happen to some of his siblings. When Whisper Gee showed Zoe his provision store she fully understood his plight. He had five feed bars left. His water was recycled waste and melt from deep in the ice crater. He was very thin as he had been rationing himself to extend his life.

Zoe then talked with Steven and told him to fully video the whole of the station for data link to earth.

Steven had been doing that and working out in his head the various stations and systems in the station. He then took one of his nanobot recorders and went into a corner to record his report of current status. With that done he then asked Zoe to have Whisper Gee open the port elevator so he could put it in to send up to the surface. At the surface opening the port would allow the reporting device to fire and rise over moon rim between the earth to shoot its data load. Zoe then took out a nutrition bar from her belt and opened it and handed it to Whisper Gee. He was effusive in his gratitude, took a bite and with surprise savored the pleasant flavor. Then Zoe touched Whisper Gee on the arm in what would be a normal gesture for her. Whisper Gee smiled with pleasure for even with a gloved hand it was the first human touch of affection he had had for many years. Zoe then explained Steven's request for the port elevator usage. Whisper Gee was happy to comply.

With the report sent in microburst laser, Zoe then began in depth study with instruction by Whisper Gee on use of the communication systems of the base. Whisper Gee had a 3D holographic monitor where he received all his instructions and training on base systems. When Zoe understood fully the interface controls with this, she instructed Steven so he could begin watching and recording all different programs. This would then be sent in another report.

While Steven was thus occupied, Zoe had Whisper Gee share his knowledge of each base system. His understanding of each system was functional but superficial. With her engineering and robotic background, she analyzed and documented in her mind the systems. She could see things that she would improve on in each, especially working with Alana. It was not long though before she could see that Whisper Gee was wearying so she asked him to show her where he bunked. When there the effects of his long near starvation, the excitement of rescue and kind human interaction, and a belly full of quality nutrition were pulling him to sleep. Zoe left him snoring quietly.

The first thing Zoe did then was to disconnect the signal sending systems so no inadvertent messages went out to the Bihaddi. Then after a brief kiss with Steven, she sent him up to home base and begin coordinating with the crew still working on the crashed Bihaddi ship. Regrettably that ship was hundreds of clicks away. She had noted all the maneuvers Whisper Gee had used to work the port and elevator. She used these to send Steven back topside. He would also gather supplies from their craft for their stay. While Steven was gone, she went through the holographic training modules. She noted how these were functional; however, limited information as to the inner workings of each system. Thus, if something broke down in the system, repairs could only be done by a superior. After all, in the Bihaddi way, slaves were expendable.

After that review she scoured the base for tools as she had noted many needed repairs and upgrades. There were none. They had been in the escape ship General Ibn had taken. When viewing the vids, she learned of the controls for the port and elevator within the base and within the port itself. Noting that she could halt the elevator topside while on surface and then come back down and in if needed. With that knowledge she suited up and went topside where she contacted Steven to have him request the tools, she would need from the Bihaddi ship salvage crew. Then she went back down to find Whisper Gee still snoring.

When Steven came back, she let him in since he had not had time to be trained on the systems yet. He brought what tools they had in their ship and food supplies. Since poor Whisper Gee did not even have a microwave to cook his food in the base, Steven had heated up some meals. He then stuffed the packages inside his suit to keep warm and brought back with him. Steven reported General Adams was very pleased with their situation. He said they would be sending up a crew to expand and upgrade the base for full time occupancy, but it would take a few weeks to get everything prepared. He further requested to be updated on any further developments, of course.

Whisper Gee was very pleased with the provisions now available and astounded to have a warm meal. Zoe, of course, gave him controlled smaller portions to allow him to adapt to the new foods and have his body be prepared to digest it as Deborah had taught her so long ago. Zoe was very pleased to have her tool kit. The faint taste of urine from the water recycler she found distasteful. While Steven went through all the training vids, she began repairing the water recycler. This took some use of what tools she had in novel ways. She did find out there was a back flush system within it and tightened the now loosened joins in several places. The end result was still a metallic tasting water, but the urine flavor was gone. Whisper Gee acted as her shadow learning as she went. He said it was like the village life when he was young where the women were in charge. She then went through the air scrubbing system. Here the numerous filters needed cleaning and there seemed to be a short circuit in one portion. This had left the air breathable but having a musty smell. With that mostly repaired and the air better she found herself yawning. Looking at her body monitoring system on her wrist, she noted that she and Steven had been working for some 26 hours. She found Steven in the bunk room where he had partitioned an area for their sleep with the bedding from their craft. Whisper Gee was also yawning. There was more to be done the next day.

CHAPTER 35

SKID STEER DESTRUCTION

General Ibn After analyzing the vids of the battle and consulting with his fellow officers came up with a strategy of using his fleet of large ships but producing many small skips loaded with pinpoint firepower to attach to each ship in multiple places for rapid deployment. They would look like ticks on a dog sucking life support until their mission deployment. They would multiply assets, provide distraction and be able to close in on and detect smaller targets and thus be able to overwhelm the attacking systems.

Getting sensors upgraded and producing the skips and establishing the attachment systems to the larger ships along with direct com systems as back up for the wireless systems and the pinpoint laser and kinetic weapons was a huge retooling and building project. Resources had to be requisitioned, engineering drawn up, asteroids harvested for space construction.

General Ibn kept up his energy by taking his usual periodic breaks to retreat to his personal quarters to perform his usual connecting ritual with the dark spirit. He would open his black hole alter and surrender himself to darkness and come away refreshed. The usual sacrifices of course would have to be offered. His attendant had been well trained on how to care for these innocents. A little blood for the everyday, a body for the big projects. The process of life being sucked out from them to fill his dark heart was his greatest pleasure. It was then he could go back to his tasks and motivate and pretend to like his men and those working with him without his snarl at these inferiors coming out. Later his attendant would have the body cooked to share to complete the ritual.

CHAPTER 36

CRACKED UP SOLUTION

When you look at an egg it appears solid. When you crack it the contents pour out. When the albumen hits the hot frying pan it changes state from liquid to solid. The skid steer of their fears would not only be the best decoy but also a container to release nanobots that would attack their ships like a virus attack on a cell. Only the nanobots had to be programmed to specifically go to the Bihaddi ships and work communicating with each other. Holographic overlay of the skid steer would hide the release and dispersal of the nanobots. Communication to the Bihaddi taunting them to surrender would come from the skid steer decoy. Of course, weaponized programmed planetary satellites would have to be targeted as well. It was unknown if there would be planetary stationed weapons systems to attack the skid steer decoy. This last did not seem to be in the Bihaddi history. Probably too inefficient with spaceships and satellites and atmospheric diffraction. Moon based weapons would have to be targeted as well. Thus, multiple levels of programming would be needed in the nanobots.

The girls presented the plan to General Adams. He liked the idea as he realistically could not see how we could match and overcome the Bihaddi using their own technology. They had established construction and deployment systems we did not have. We had the ability to make mockup skid steers. We now had to the ability to deliver them to distant star systems. We had the ability to load the decoy skid steer with stuff. We had the ability to program and build in communication systems within the decoy skid steer. What we did not have were the programmed nanobots and the overlay hologram technologies. Delivery of the skid steer would need oversight as each situation would present unique parameters. If the Bihaddi chose to surrender upon communication from the skid steer, then that also needed local oversight and diplomatic decision making.

Barbara, Alana, and Zoe worked with task forces at MIT and NASA on engineering nanobots. To have them be small enough to avoid detection, yet able to do the various functions of seeking out appropriate targets, having destructive effect on the target, and communicating with each other and the oversight of the officer who brought them, they had to have limited data platforms they shared when in contact with other nanobots. Their processing platforms would multiply as they amalgamated in 10s, 100s, 1000s, etc. They would stream out from the skid steer in small groups that would agglomerate on their target, begin boring, and deliver destructive charge when in an appropriate location or on command from the delivering officer who would be well separated and camouflaged directing the attack.

It was expected that the Bihaddi would upon sighting the skid steer immediately attack, pinpointing their weapons on the small target. Thus, it was the payload of nanobots would have to be released almost immediately and separated from the skid steer decoy. The very small nature and dispersion of the nanobots was expected to protect the vast majority of them from Bihaddi attack direct or inadvertent. Extra nanobots would be kept on the pilot's base ship with preprogrammed instructions for different scenarios to be selected by the pilot of the dark shielded delivery vehicle.

Production went into effect with Alana and Zoe working with assigned engineers creating micro robotic production lines first creating the tools for mass production and then making the nanobots, programming them, and loading them in their delivery containers. The skid steer decoys were created with compartments for the nanobots and communication platforms to deliver their message as well as the holographic overlay system for full effect. Barbara's father was again used as the face of skid steer man in the video projections.

Production went faster than expected with 3D printing and robotic programming precision and production. Training the pilots, who were all volunteers, in the controls of the ships was first done via computer gaming, then mockups, and finally short hops to the moon delivering supplies to the moon base and bringing back persons and equipment from the crashed Bihaddi ship and moon station. Whisper Gee had been brought down to earth where he had to undergo months of rehab to strengthen his bone and muscles to earths greater gravity. Though he would have gladly continued to follow in a puppyish fashion his favorite person, Ms. Zoe, he knew he did not have the strength once in earth gravity. He did continue studying how things worked as he had a great fascination with mechanics. He even put up with all the fuss of the doctors taking samples and examining him multiple times over the months.

CHAPTER 37

CALL TO QUARTERS

With everything ready, coordinates logged in, programming fully updated, personnel fully trained and ready to go it was time. General Ibn was in the process of making his final big offering on his dark altar when it was sighted and the clarion call to quarters sounded. The sacrifice process was halted, and he ran through his flash cleaner directly to the command platform. The little ships were already deployed, and his men were all performing as they had trained. There were three of their strange ships blipping on the screen so far. A message had been broadcast from them in clear Bihaddi warning them to surrender. This had caused a hesitation among the Bihaddi ranks. Upon gaining awareness of this General Ibn went manic with rage. He stormed to the com officer, pounded the com control to general broadcast and ordered all units to fire on the usurpers. The decoys flashed into superheated gas. General Ibn watched gloating as they flashed. Then three more of those hated ships appeared. Targeting was redirected and again a satisfying flash. But now something sinister seemed to be happening. At first a few of his skip units were going dark. He thought this might have been caused by debris from the destruction of the foreign ships as they were closest to the targets. Then similar reports of some kind of dark paint attaching to the skips were coming in just before they went dark. The pattern of attack was moving outward to his ships from the targets and his men were starting to panic. Another three foreign ships appeared now between his fleet and habitable system planet. Again the message to surrender was received. Again, targeting was directed, and the invader ships destroyed but what was that on the sensors? "Officer Auminst enlarge that vid on the closest invader." Ordered General Ibn. There it was. Something dark oozing out of the ships. Where was it going? "Enhance that vid and sensor readings on that dark ooze coming from that ship, Officer Auminst." commanded General Ibn. As they followed the ooze something else blipped in the background. "Stop there. Can you enhance that more?" General Ibn could feel something there. What was it? Dark on dark. Coldly he commanded, "Target that. Fire." The flaring of shield arcing with laser fire light up the sky. As it did more black ooze was lit up contrasting with the white light of shield arcing. Then the shield was overcome by the power of his laser cannons and the dark object went red then dark again with starlight shining through the middle. Then he knew. Almost all his skips had gone dark now and his larger ships were sending distress signals now. Where there others out there?

General Ibn gave the command to all remaining ships to set sensors to maximum and search the surrounding sky for stars being blocked out and to fire at that target. There was some firing from his saber class frigates and even then, two flares of shield arcing but laser power cut short, and the frigate went dark without the red of before. There were very few skips left now and they were doing evasive maneuvers. The saber class frigates were scattering. He could hear confusion and panic in the comm broadcasts between ships. That damn ooze. What was that? His lighting was flickering now, and he could sense how his men were panicked. What he did not sense was the junior watch officer on deck with the pocket laser. The flash of light in the darkening room he sensed. The burning hole in his head were his nose used to be he sensed. As his senses went dark, he felt the pull of the black hole he had worshipped for so many years. But this was not a loving embrace. This was the unbearable weight of all the horrors he had committed, all the suffering he had caused, all the killing he had done. The scales tipped and he was judged. The sentence he gave himself, annihilation.

CHAPTER 38

BRINGING THINGS TO LIGHT

The third of the Bihaddi fleet that was left surrendered. Each ship had varying amounts of damage from the nanobots. The ten officers who had volunteered in their black ovoid ships had varying amounts of knowledge of the Bihaddi language. The translation programs in their helmets were translating rapidly but there were multiple speakers in each Bihaddi ship. Mutiny had occurred on many of the ships with younger officers taking control and effecting surrender. Initially video conferencing with each ship was one ship to ship through Barbara's father hologram. Then when that programmed interaction was exceeded by the complexity of situation the officers turned on their vid com channel stating they had been delegated to further interface with the survivors. There was great fear among the Bihaddi personnel as each had watched the total destruction of the first fleet. Many of the ships had life support systems failing and their time of survival was limited. Admiral Downey was the chief officer of the black ovoid fleet. At that point he instructed his fleet officers to instruct the nanobots to repair life support systems on the Bihaddi ships but to keep weapons systems nonfunctional. He then had the command translated and broadcast to the Bihaddi forces. He then introduced himself as the commander of the United Earth Defense Fleet. His first command was that all comm systems be opened to allow open monitoring. With this in place, his processing systems listened to the command deck communications. He also had the back up of nanobots monitoring conversations in various other parts of the Bihaddi ships. This last most likely unknown to them. Admiral Downey was pleased to note no signs of continued resistance.

Admiral Downey understood that his little fleet did not have the power to tug the now drifting Bihaddi ships. Thus, his second order to the remaining Bihaddi forces was to present him with a plan for capture of each dead Bihaddi ship and setting up tow systems or attachment to the functional ships. He gave them a time frame for presenting their plan of two hours. This created a buzz of communication between the on-deck officers of each ship and then between ships. A reasonable plan was presented to Admiral Downey at the two-hour mark and that was implemented immediately. Admiral Downey then had Lieutenant Austin Longhorse, the most proficient of his officers in the Bihaddi language and in reading their body language (he had been dating Barbara for one year) dock with the Bihaddi command ship. Due to quarantine issues he had to remain in his suit, but he could show his face through his suit and see through his visor as he went on deck. This allowed the Bihaddi officers and personnel see his face. Of course, there was also supermicro nanotech in his suit that provided protection if he was attacked. Thank goodness that was not needed. Once aboard Lieutenant Longhorse could read the fear of the young officers in control. He learned how General Ibn had been killed and the senior officers had been seized and locked in the brig. They had been very loyal to General Ibn. There was no way General Ibn was going to surrender. He had a special escape pod his command chair could drop into in an instant. He would have sacrificed all of them and think nothing of it as he had done with his previous fleet. His body still sat slumped in his command chair. There had been no time yet to dispose of it.

Lieutenant Longhorse then sought to calm the fear in these young men. He told them we have no desire to rule you, but we will not allow others to subjugate us. He told them we have found that freedom for each allows each to find their way. That with freedom life has a way of pushing those who will strive for the best, those who will give of themselves, to thrive. When this happens all live better lives. There was confusion in the eyes of some and a flicker of hope in the eyes of all. With that he took command of the ship and began directing the salvage mission.

It was only after getting some of the kinks worked out of docking damaged Bihaddi ships to the functional ones and gathering them in to rendezvous with the stations that had built the fleet did he finally have a moment to himself. His suit was beginning to smell stale and sour. The men on board seemed competent in their duties and were gaining respect for his gentle but firm command. Further he had shown innovation in solving the many problems of docking the many ships that had been incapacitated. About half of the personnel aboard the damaged ships had managed to survive and were very grateful for the assistance as they were facing imminent death. At this point, Lieutenant Longhorse was asked by the Lieutenant Giurf, the commanding officer of the command ship under him, to come see General Ibn's quarters. He had received a report from one of the orderlies who were cleaning the ship and assessing damage from the battle about shocking things there. Lieutenant Longhorse displayed the ship demographics to map out the General's quarters and noted an anomaly. There was a certain area that seemed blurred out next to that cabin and there was another one attached to the cabin of the general's personal attendant. When he and Lieutenant Giurf entered the cabin seemed normal enough. Then they entered the attendant's cabin and found he had committed suicide and left the door to the unknown area open where cages with the freshly dead bodies of children were found. It was obvious the attendant had been caring for the children and had slaughtered them when his general had been killed. Lieutenant Giurf was clearly shocked, and Lieutenant Longhorse could clearly see that he was struggling to keep from vomiting as he himself was. Lieutenant Longhorse ordered full vid documentation of this be recorded by Lieutenant Giurf as he also had his own system record. Then they went back to General Ibn's cabin and began searching for the access to the hidden area. There at the back of his closet was a finger scanner. Accessing a bit of Barbara's holographic programming Lieutenant Longhorse recreated the right thumbprint of the general and had the scan read that. A door opened to a black room that was well lit, where an alter with a child's body lay. The blood was drying now but the horror of it was too much for Lieutenant Giurf who had to step back and vomit.

Going back to the attendant's room they found his personal log. Lieutenant Longhorse had now patched into the comm link system to broadcast not only between ships but also to the planets in the system what he and Lieutenant Giurf were seeing. The bodies and altar were now widely broadcast, and the attendant's personal log was shown with promise that a full disclosure of its contents would follow. Admiral Downey at that point cut in to fully publish that he was authorized as representative of the United Earth Defense Fleet that these behaviors by General Ibn and his attendant both shock and disgust. Further we come not to enslave, but to provide a path to self-governance and freedom within appropriate boundaries. It is our desire to set up trading systems and communication that all may learn and thrive. Further in order to help all understand the cultures of our world we will begin broadcasting uncensored videos from the various cultures with translation for you. With that Admiral Downey cut out and began playing the preselected videos that

Barbara and the girls had selected as the best introduction to earth cultures.

It was shortly thereafter that Lieutenant Longhorse had the great pleasure of meeting a docking United Earth Defense Fleet ship that had just come into the system. From it Barbara came into the command center. They had taken Bill's advice and secretly made a spaceship similar but better than what they had come to earth in and then duplicated it so each had their own. This had been relatively easy using Hermosa's research on scattering iron rich red clay dust in the middle of the Pacific Ocean to promote phytoplankton. This was to continue research on how adding the key nutrient of iron would increase food production in the ocean and sequester CO2 reducing global warming. The whole process was set up robotically using antigravitation systems and simply mining a small amount of red clay from our ranch. All equipment for the transport of the few tons of clay were made on the ranch by these young ladies and oversight was a bit lax with all the preparations to face the Bihaddi fleet. There was plenty of money and supplies between patent royalties and cryptocurrency mining. The robotic systems were intact at the ranch and proper facilities for construction were built as valuable research was being performed here. There was hope they would find family members upon return to Aarumw and also the need to check on their brave men.

When Barbara saw Lieutenant Longhorse with the dark circles and drawn look from the stress of battle and having to take command afterwards, she gave him the crisp command of a woman who knows and sincerely cares for her man, to board her ship and get out of that suit and get some rest. The Bihaddi officers were surprised at Lieutenant Longhorse's crisp reply of yes sir. Then she introduced herself in fluent Bihaddi to the ship's officers explaining how she was from planet Aarumw and that she had returned to help her people regain their freedom and dignity. She explained how she and her sisters had escaped the Bihaddi and the good they had seen where people were allowed freedom and their accountability of those in positions of power. She further explained how she knew each of the men who had come with the United Earth Defense Fleet and knew the quality and virtue of each. The concepts of conquer pillage and rape were primitive, destructive, and debasing of the perpetrator and the victim, scarring each for life. What ever was gained by such actions was tainted and those who taught others such behavior was acceptable were aligning themselves with evil.

Barbara then told Auston Longhorse how she had come with Alana and Zoe, each in separate ships they had made to secretly return to their birth planet. They had hopes of seeing family again and freeing their people, also it was important to for her to see him. Their ships were smaller and faster without the weapons systems. She then told him how Zoe went to the ship Steven now commanded to see him on his off-duty cycle before their descent to the planet surface. Also, Zoe had hidden her pregnancy from all but Barbara who knew from the first touch.

Conner had been able to hide the extent of his burns from the momentary laser blast while in his suit as he commanded the frigate assigned to him. It was when Alana heard his voice at his surprise with her arrival that she knew something was wrong. He had been very busy supervising repairs on the frigate and the docking and repair of skips. The crew he supervised was rotating shifts and when not on shift had been watching the vids provided by the United Earth Defense Fleet with fascination. It was now time to start the fourth shift and Conner had yet to rest. Alana immediately had his second take command and commanded him to her vessel. Once inside and out of the suit she saw the red of his burns and how his red hair and beard were singed. The med systems in the suit had treated his burns well, but he was still blistering on his cheeks. Between his exhaustion and injuries, he slept almost immediately. It was only later he learned he had slept for some 16 hours. He awoke with a start from a dream where his eyes were about to be poked with hot irons to see his beloved Alana above him. Holding his hands firmly but gently she kept him from rubbing his eyes. Then with great care she gently put drops in his eyes to sooth them. Now fully awake he sat up, a bit stiff but feeling much better and hungry. Over their meal Alana reported the current status.

Fleet stats was steady with the last of the skips and all other ships now attached or in tow to the above planet dry dock. They had lost one ship and felt the loss of their good friend Captain Fredrick and his second. His dry humor and bad puns would be missed even if they were often groaners. Whisper Gee had somehow managed to get on Zoe's ship and refused to wear a space suit when transferring to Stephen's assigned frigate. Some of the older stewards had even recognized him. His telling the story of his life to them and how he was treated by the earth people had a calming and reassuring effect on the common sailors. Admiral Downey had learned of Barbara, Alana, and Zoe's arrival and though surprised was pleased to have planetary ambassadors while he remained with the fleet. There were some disturbances reported planet-side as most of the Bihaddi leaders and appointees had been killed or imprisoned either with the defeat of the Bihaddi fleet or the exposure of General Ibn and his attendant. With the videos they broadcast and now with some short clips of Whisper Gee there seemed a sigh of relief among most of the people.

It was now a time to heal and rebuild a better world on Aarumw. Hermosa had not come because she could not leave her research and she could not leave Victor Cortez her associate and fellow researcher. Somehow after 12 hours of working together they wanted to stay with each other the rest of the day.

Admiral Downey, Barbara, Lieutenant Longhorse, Alana, Conner, Zoe and Steven knew the Bihaddi had other worlds and there was much more to do.

CHAPTER 39

DISTANT OBSERVATIONS

Far away on planet Seweruez, Bihaddi origin planet intelligence was coming in about General Ibn's recent battles. The loss of two fleets was a setback but the flow of assets from the three systems was intact and with use of infiltration and indoctrination the plan continues. Gather the information. Pull in the assets. Study the culture, corrupt the culture, know the tactics, and destroy from within. Use tribal ideation with self-righteousness and fanaticism to justify good people following the dark path of the Bihaddi. All things go to the black hole.

The end—or should I say more to come in the next book ....

ABOUT THE AUTHOR

William Mark Corff, DC, I was born Oklahoma City, the 7th son and 13th child of Barbara and Nicholas Corff, graduated from Oklahoma City University and went on to Parker College of Chiropractic.

I went on to live and practice for 6 years in Paradise Valley, Montana where my address with the post office was the Blue House behind the old saloon.

With the divorce from my wife, I came back to Oklahoma where I worked in various practices, met my second wife and lived in Ponca City, Oklahoma for several years and retired from practice.

I then taught high school science for two years at

the small town of Pond Creek. Afraid I was not very good at that, due to going through a second divorce and taking care of my newborn son at the time.

Regarding marriage third time is good as I have been with Deborah for over 20 years now living on our horse ranch south of Cushing, Oklahoma.

We raise sport horses and have been doing medical transcription at home over the net for 20 years. Basically, we started here with lots of potential and bootstrapped our way.

Writing was always a desire and dabs of poetry might be heard coming from my mouth if I did not know you were within ear shot. I talk to my horses and animals and sometimes they understand. Mostly they convey love and the need for good food.

I hope what I write will be food for your thoughts.

www.ingramcontent.com/pod-product-compliance
Lightning Source LLC
La Vergne TN
LVHW091326150826
845673LV00006B/1785

* 9 7 9 8 3 5 5 4 8 2 8 1 7 *